"What kind of man is he?" Carter asked

He looked deeply into her eyes before continuing, "Believe me, if I'd found the woman I wanted to spend the rest of my life with, I wouldn't take the chance of her getting away from me by leaving her free to find someone else."

The amber stare of his eyes seemed to have an almost hypnotic effect on her.

"In fact," he went on, "I'd fill her life and her thoughts and her bed so completely that she wouldn't *want* to find someone else."

Elspeth gaped at him. "If you're suggesting that I want to find someone else," she accused recklessly, "then let me tell you that you're wrong. I am perfectly content with Peter."

"Content." His dark eyebrows climbed sharply. "Contentment, my dear Elspeth, is for old age, not youth."

PENNY JORDAN was constantly in trouble in school because of her inability to stop daydreaming—especially during French lessons. In her teens, she was an avid romance reader, although it didn't occur to her to try writing one herself until she was older. "My first half dozen attempts ended up ingloriously," she remembers, "but I persevered, and one manuscript was finished." She plucked up the courage to send it to a publisher, convinced her book would be rejected. It wasn't, and the rest is history! Penny is married and lives in Cheshire.

Penny Jordan's striking mainstream novel *Power Play* quickly became a *New York Times* bestseller. She followed that success with *Silver,* a story of ambition, passion and intrigue. Penny's latest blockbuster, *The Hidden Years,* lays bare the choices all women face in their search for love.

Books by Penny Jordan

Don't miss any of our special offers. Write to us at the following address for information on our newest releases.

Harlequin Reader Service
P.O. Box 1397, Buffalo, NY 14240
Canadian address: P.O. Box 603,
Fort Erie, Ont. L2A 5X3

PENNY JORDAN

a kind of madness

Harlequin Books

TORONTO • NEW YORK • LONDON
AMSTERDAM • PARIS • SYDNEY • HAMBURG
STOCKHOLM • ATHENS • TOKYO • MILAN
MADRID • WARSAW • BUDAPEST • AUCKLAND

Harlequin Presents first edition May 1992
ISBN 0-373-11456-7

Original hardcover edition published in 1990
by Mills & Boon Limited

A KIND OF MADNESS

CHAPTER ONE

'SO YOU'RE leaving for Cheshire this evening. Exactly when do your parents sail?' Peter asked.

They were having lunch at their usual restaurant, equidistant from Elspeth's bank and Peter's chambers. Both of them had agreed early on in their relationship that it made much more sense for them to fix a couple of days per week when they could lunch together, rather than committing too many of their precious busy evenings to developing their relationship.

That was one of the things that made their relationship so harmonious: they both had the same goals, the same outlook on life—the same firm and practical outlook. Not for them the heady, and so often destructive and exhausting passion of others. Which made it all the more difficult to understand why her parents, instead of approving of Peter, seemed almost to treat their relationship as a joke.

Of course, her parents and Peter were worlds apart; her parents were her parents, but one had to admit they *were* a trifle unorthodox in their attitude to the things that Peter considered important—one could almost say a little careless and feckless in their outlook on life, never treating it with the seriousness they should. Look at the way now that her father, having sold the farm and bought a smallholding, instead of investing the remainder of the money in some safe manner which would give them a good income, was insisting on taking her mother off to Egypt and then the Greek islands for a two-month holiday.

Really, the pair of them could be as irrational and as irresponsible as a pair of children at times. It was a good job that she was around to keep an eye on them. When her father had first sold the farm, she had heaved a small sigh of relief. She loved her parents, of course, but the farm and its demands had sometimes proved to be a small bone of contention between Peter and herself. The very first time she had introduced him to her parents, he had generously tried to point out to her father how foolish he was in trying to continue farming in the outdated traditional method her father had favoured, when he could have made the farm so much more profitable by using modern intensive methods. Peter had only been trying to help, and it had been unfortunate that her father felt so strongly about retaining the traditional methods of agriculture, and that Peter hadn't realised that he had been treading almost on hallowed ground by arguing against them.

When her mother had first told her they were selling the farm, she had been pleased, envisaging a safe, comfortable life for them in a pleasant, easily run house in one of the very attractive local Cheshire villages, but to her shock what her parents had bought was a small and extremely run-down smallholding, which they had told her with enthusiasm and excitement they intended to use to raise organically grown vegetable crops.

Her mother, Elspeth remembered, had been bubbling over with eagerness for the project, explaining that they had already canvassed the very popular local restaurants, with which Cheshire was well supplied, to ensure that there was a ready market for their produce.

Elspeth had been dragged down to view the appalling wreck of a cottage, which looked fit only for demolition, and the flat, overgrown paddock that went with it.

She had tried to talk her parents out of such a crazy venture, her heart sinking when she'd realised they had made up their minds. The frustration of not being able to make them see that their money would give them a far better return if it was invested had sent her back to London with a pounding headache, and the unpleasant sinking sensation that Peter would consider her to have failed in not persuading them to change their minds. Why couldn't her parents be more like Peter's? His father and mother had retired to a small south coast town, where they played golf and bridge. They had an immaculate detached bungalow with smooth green lawns and well-disciplined flower-beds. No pets were allowed in the Holmes household, no cats with unexpected litters of kittens, no rough stray dogs with large muddy paws and hairy coats ... no parrots who called out the most appallingly rude things when one was least expecting it. She still blushed to remember how, the first time she had taken Peter home, the parrot which her mother had originally been taking care of for a friend, and which had somehow or other lingered on to become a permanent house guest, had flown on to Peter's shoulder and bitten quite sharply at his ear before remarking in a voice which sounded uncomfortably like her mother's, 'Oh, dear, such a shame. Pious Peter... Pious Peter...'

'Well, perhaps once they get back from this holiday they'll come to see sense and sell up. I must say, Elspeth, I do find your parents rather...' Peter frowned and studied his plate as though unable to find the words to describe his reaction to her family, while Elspeth hung her head in acknowledgement of his criticism.

It wasn't until she had come to live in London that she had realised how eccentric and unusual her home life was. Having a father who was a farmer had caused a few amused raised eyebrows, but not too much other comment in the high-powered world of merchant banking. It was only after she'd made the mistake of taking a colleague home with her one Christmas that she'd made the humiliating discovery of how very odd and amusing her family was to others.

She had reacted instinctively on learning that Sophy, the other girl, had had nowhere to spend Christmas, inviting her to return to Cheshire with her, knowing quite well that another body would hardly be noticed in the crowd that her mother always drew around her. Having produced only one child, her mother had gone on to make up for this by maternally adopting every chance waif and stray she could, both of the human and animal varieties, and so it was that the farm had abounded with pet lambs turned aggressive and demanding sheep, goats who could never be milked, chickens too old to lay but whose necks could never be wrung, sheep-dogs who only dreamed lazily of sheep in their old age as they huddled up to the Aga, a collection of barn cats who never hunted—although thankfully in those days the parrot had not been in evidence.

Sophy had seemed to fit in so well with her family that it had come as a double shock to walk into the staff-room behind her and discover her entertaining a crowd of their fellow employees by telling them in her high-pitched Sloane Ranger voice about the chaos of the Turner household.

Elspeth had never felt so humiliated in her life. She had resolved there and then that, in the future, no one would ever be able to humiliate her or laugh at her in that kind of way again.

When her mother had asked gently why she no longer brought any friends home with her when she came back from London, she had quietly and firmly avoided a direct answer. From then on her home life and her career were two separate things.

After that she had been cautious about where and with whom she made friends. She had swapped her room at the small, crowded flat she'd shared with four other girls and had found herself a lone bedsitter.

Having more time to spend on her own had given her the opportunity to concentrate on her exams, so that when Sophy had been simpering over the engagement ring she had managed to extract from an up-and-coming bank clerk, she, Elspeth, had been quietly receiving the congratulations of her management on the excellence of her exam results.

While her colleagues had opted for the glamour and high-powered pressure of the dealing-room, she had set her sights in a different direction, cautiously looking ahead to the future, and equally cautiously deciding to leave the world of mainstream banking for the more specialised arena of merchant banking.

Here it seemed she had found her niche. She loved the meticulous, quiet, thoughtful concentration needed for such work; she liked being out of the public eye, working behind the scenes; and she was rewarded for her diligence with a good salary which had enabled her to buy her own small dockside apartment and to run a neat, economical car.

She had met Peter when he'd moved into an adjoining apartment. They had soon discovered how much they had in common. Unlike other couples, they had decided against moving into one shared apartment. After all, when they eventually decided to marry, by selling the two apartments they would have sufficient profit to enable them to buy a sensible London house which would be convenient for both their offices.

Later, when they had children, they might decide to move a little way out of London, somewhere convenient for the M4 and healthy for bringing up children. Yes, she and Peter had their lives all properly planned... Not for her the careless insouciance of her parents, who always left so much to chance.

When she had once gently chided her mother for this, the latter had replied firmly, 'Elspeth, we like surprises, even the bad ones. I can't understand how you can bear to have your life so carefully mapped out, every move planned. My dear, think how boring it will be...'

She had subdued the small, rebellious voice inside her which had found astoundingly that her mother had been right, reminding herself of her humiliation at the hands of the insufferable Sophy. That was never going to happen to her again—nor to her children. They would have parents whom they would know would never do anything to embarrass them. She would never forget the awful humiliation of that day...the mockery and laughter of her colleagues...the cruelty of Sophy, who had exaggerated her parents' soft Cheshire accents just sufficiently to make them sound almost unbelievably bucolic, who had described in loving, cruel detail the plethora of cats, dogs and livestock that had run riot in and around the old farmhouse, who had mocked her mother's somewhat casual attitude to the kind of housework that involved having a home in which nothing looked as though it was ever out of place. Even now it made her squirm to remember.

'I'll try to drive up to Cheshire for your second weekend there,' she heard Peter saying, and automatically switched her thoughts from the past and back to the present.

Three weeks ago, just before her mother had telephoned and dropped her bombshell that she and Elspeth's father had decided more or less on the spur of the moment to take a long holiday, Elspeth's boss had sent for her, and had told her almost

severely that it was time she used some of the eight
weeks of leave that was due to her.

Thoroughly alarmed that he might have been
suggesting a fall in the standard of her work,
Elspeth had protested that she didn't need a holiday,
that she enjoyed her work so much.

'Yes, Elspeth, I know and I do sympathise, but
the board has issued instructions that, praise-
worthy though they consider it that our staff are
so conscientious, in this day and age with so many
stress-related illnesses their staff must take their due
allocation of holiday leave. Our personnel department tell me that it is over two years since you
had a break of longer than three or four days.

'The board has asked me to provide them with
a list of all those members of staff who have more
than one year's allocation of leave built up.

'The view of the board is that a healthy staff
member with a well-rounded attitude to life will in
the long run serve the bank better than, to use a
current term, a "workaholic".

'I think you will agree that, in these circumstances, it might be as well if you could find a way
of using up some of your built-up leave. I do sympathise, Elspeth, but the Livingstone contract is all
but wound up, and unless you have something very
pressing to attend to...'

Elspeth had shaken her head, her heart sinking,
knowing that she had had no possible excuse for
not taking her boss's advice.

When he had added a further blow, telling her
that he expected her to take at least four weeks'
leave, she had left his office feeling almost as sick

with shock as she had done on that never to be forgotten occasion when she had overheard Sophy's malicious description of her parents and home.

Had anyone told Elspeth that she was an extremely sensitive, almost over-sensitive young woman, whose emotions and self-confidence were easily bruised, she would have reacted with astonishment and dismissal. She considered herself to be one of that new breed of women who had managed to tame and control all those dangerously subversive feminine traits which had told so badly against her sex in the past.

Not for her sentimentality and the weakness of allowing her emotions to rule her head; not for her the folly of falling in love, of submitting herself to the pain of allowing another human being to become so important to her that he was the focus of her whole world. No, she preferred to put her faith, her trust in something far more dependable—like her work. Of course she wanted to marry, to have children, and in Peter she considered she had found the perfect mate: someone who felt about life exactly as she did.

They considered themselves an established couple, even though she wasn't wearing an engagement ring, even though they were not as yet lovers. Peter was old-fashioned in such things, and she was glad of it. These days, when one heard and read of the appalling consequences of sexual freedom and promiscuity, it was reassuring to meet a man who considered his health more important than the satisfaction of physical desire. There had been one previous serious relationship in Peter's life, a girl at university, but that was in the past. And as for her...

Elspeth moved uncomfortably in her chair. Her virginity was something she preferred not to dwell on. It had been the source of enough mirth among the other girls she had flat-shared with when the local office of her bank had first transferred her to London, and she had been too hurt and too proud to explain to the others that it was very difficult to enter into a purely physical fling with the careless abandon they seemed to favour when one lived and worked in a small country town, where everyone knew everyone else, and where at the first sign of her attempting to do any such thing the gossips would be having a field day.

And then by the time she had moved to London she had felt too shy, too self-conscious to remedy things. After Sophy—strange how she always thought of her life as before Sophy and after Sophy—she had curled up into herself, not trusting herself to form any new relationships with anyone, male or female.

But now there was Peter, and if she sometimes found his insistence that they did not sleep together, his reluctance to touch her at all except to give her the odd very chaste and brief kiss, somewhat lacking in passion, she comforted herself with the knowledge that she would have found a man who was far more openly and demandingly sexual very off-putting indeed.

No, Peter was right for her, and once they were married of course things would be different. As it was, their careers took up so much of their time that it was hardly surprising that Peter wasn't keen to rush on their marriage. After all, as he had pointed out to her recently, the terrible events of the autumn of '87, when the markets had fallen so drastically and so many of their peers had lost their jobs, had had a disastrous effect on the property market, which had still not recovered, and it would be foolish for them to make marriage plans and to sell their flats until it had done so.

She had agreed wholeheartedly with him, but it had niggled her none the less the last time her mother had rung up to have had to explain that no, she and Peter had not made any wedding arrangements as yet.

It was the purpose of that phone call which was the subject of their lunchtime discussion today.

Her mother had been thrilled about the planned holiday, but she had been concerned about leaving her menagerie. 'Fortunately, Carter has offered to take over and look after things for us... You remember Carter, don't you, Elspeth?'

She did, but wished she did not. Carter MacDonald was her aunt's stepson, but he had already been an adult when her aunt had married his father, and his visits to the farmhouse had consequently been very rare. What she did remember about him was that she had found him rather overpowering. Almost eight years her senior, she had first met him the summer her aunt had married his father. He had just finished university at the time and had been waiting to hear if his application to work in scientific crop research for Third World countries had been successful. Her feelings towards him had been so ambiguous that when her mother had mentioned his name alarm bells had started to ring wildly in her cautious brain, especially when she couldn't seem to explain what Carter was doing in Cheshire when he was supposed to be working in America.

Gently she had tried to caution her mother against leaving a man who was after all almost a stranger to them in charge of the smallholding because, for all her own objections and fears, she had had to admit that her parents were making an outstanding success of their venture, with the vegetables they produced being in constant demand from prestigious local restaurants and hotels. Indeed, so successful was it becoming that they were being pressed to expand, to erect more greenhouse tunnels and to buy more land. Their accounts, when they had proudly shown them to her, had stunned her. She had had no idea it was possible to make so much money from producing organically grown food.

When she had said as much to Peter he had lectured her reprovingly, pointing out that with the move to a far more 'green' environment it was obvious that her parents' produce would sell well.

And now they were jeopardising the whole thing by lightheartedly taking off for two months and leaving their precious business in the hands of a man about whom they knew virtually nothing at all.

Not so, her mother had objected when she had pointed these facts out to her. In the past few months they had got to know Carter very well indeed. It was true that initially he had merely been looking them up out of good manners, having returned to England after a spell working in America. But it seemed that now for some reason he was seriously considering settling in Cheshire and that, moreover, he had plans to enter a similar line of business to her parents', so that he had both the experience and the inclination to take over the running of the business while they were away.

Elspeth had found all this highly suspicious. Her memories of Carter were of a tall, thin male with a shock of overlong dark hair who had seemed very adult to her teenage self, someone who had made her very aware of her own immaturity. Her mother was even talking enthusiastically about him buying a small farm due to come up for sale next to their own land, so that the two ventures could be run as one, but her parents were so innocent . . . so naïve. They couldn't see what Peter had been quick to point out to her—something she had not realised at first herself—that it might well be that Carter *did* intend to start up a business, a business which would be in direct competition to their own—and what better way to get a head start than by destroying their business while they were away and he was in charge?

Of course, she had known immediately it would be useless to point this out to her mother. For one thing, she knew that her mother would only laugh and dismiss Peter's suspicions as unthinkable.

She had talked the whole thing over with him and he had pointed out further aspects of the situation which had not occurred to her: namely,

that not only might Carter not take adequate care
of her parents' venture, but that he might actually
deliberately try to undermine everything they had
built up. 'After all, if he is serious about setting up
in competition to them...' he had gone on.

Shocked, Elspeth had initially demurred, but
Peter had insisted he was right. She had immediately wanted to warn her parents, but had
known that they would not take her warning
seriously. They seemed to have taken Carter to their
hearts, almost as though he were a long-lost son,
not someone who was barely related to them at all
if one discounted her aunt's marriage to his father.

A sensation which she had refused to admit as
jealousy had struggled for life inside her—a
sensation which she had immediately squashed. But
then had come her boss's announcement that she
must take some leave, and she had immediately
suggested to Peter that it might be as well for her
to kill two birds with one stone by taking her leave
and by spending it in Cheshire, where she could
keep a firm eye on any Machiavellian attempts by
Carter to undermine her parents' business.

Peter had immediately agreed with her decision.
She had rung her parents that evening, announcing
that she had some leave due and that *she* was free
to stand in for them while she was on holiday.

At first her mother had seemed surprisingly
unenthusiastic, almost as though she didn't *want*
her at home, and her ire and suspicions had grown
when she had later learned that it was Carter who
had told her parents that that kind of sacrifice on

her part was unnecessary, and that he was sure she would much prefer to spend her leave with Peter.

Not so, she had returned firmly. And in the end her mother had thanked her and accepted her decision, although even then she had not seemed very confident of Elspeth's ability to take charge. Which was foolish, surely. After all, her parents had a small staff who did the day-to-day routine work. Elspeth was used to dealing with underlings, having a small department under her at the bank, and surely a well-educated, mature woman of twenty-seven would have no trouble at all in running one very small smallholding for a period of one month.

And so she had planned everything. She would drive down to Cheshire three days ahead of her parents' departure so that she could familiarise herself with their routine, and make sure that Carter knew that any interference on his part would not be welcome.

It was a pity that he was living in the area while he looked around for a suitable property of his own, but if he turned up at her parents' smallholding she would make it more than plain to him that, in their absence, he was *not* a welcome guest.

As she listened to Peter telling her about his latest case, she smothered the uncomfortable feeling that if her parents had made Carter welcome in their home as a member of the family, they would be highly embarrassed if she refused to do the same. She reflected crossly that it was high time she overcame these rebellious and unwanted weaknesses which more properly she ought to have left behind her when she'd left home.

Her parents were a warm-hearted couple, whose naïveté about the realities of life and the human race were all very well in the context of a small rural village where they had been known all their lives, but the world had changed dramatically since her parents were young, and it frightened her sometimes how little they seemed to realise that fact.

Take the time she had got off the London train in Chester, only to discover that her mother had befriended a solitary and extremely hairy young man who had got off an earlier train, and even worse that she had practically invited him home for the weekend. One only had to pick up a paper to realise the danger of befriending strangers.

Not that Carter was a stranger precisely, but his motives were very suspect, as Peter had wisely pointed out to her. In fact Peter had rather chided her because she herself had not seen that danger immediately.

Truth to tell, she had been inclined to become more indignant about the way Carter seemed to have wormed his way into her parents' affections and become an established part of their lives—so much so that the last time she had gone home, when mercifully he had been away visiting friends for the weekend, the parrot had shrieked unrelentingly, 'Where's Carter? I want Carter. Now there's a man,' accompanying this statement with a barrage of wolf-whistles and other equally unsavoury remarks.

It was not Jasper's fault, her mother had apologised. The parrot had had three homes before being dumped on her parents; one of these being a Manchester pub, no doubt frequented by the kind of men who thought nothing of whistling at women and making fulsome remarks about their physical endowments.

Peter had remarked on their return drive to London that he sincerely hoped the bird would have met its demise by the time their children came along. 'It's that kind of thing that exerts the worst possible influence on young children,' he had informed Elspeth.

Even worse, as she cringingly remembered, had been the reaction of Peter's mother when he had described the parrot's excesses to her the following weekend.

Peter was scrupulous about making sure that they never visited one set of parents without visiting the other, and if sometimes she had the unnerving feeling that he was doling out these duty visits with more parsimony than real emotion, she kept these unwanted thoughts firmly subdued.

Peter's parents were nothing like her own. Peter's mother was a wonderful housewife. Her furniture gleamed with polish, her kitchen floor could literally be dined off, and if Elspeth sometimes noticed the stiff formality of her visits there, the immaculate tidiness of the small sitting-room with its furniture that was both uncomfortable and almost too tidily arranged, she smothered her feelings and concentrated instead on reminding herself that once they were married Peter would no doubt expect her to maintain the same high standards attained by his mother.

That would be a challenge, but Elspeth reminded herself that the modern career woman thrived on such challenges, skilfully balancing the needs of career, home and family, and in doing so winning the admiration of everyone around her.

Mrs Holmes did not really approve of wives who worked. In her day making a home had been enough to keep any woman contented, but on the other hand she agreed with Peter that the additional income Elspeth earned would contribute welcomely to the family budget. There had even been a moment when Peter's mother had suggested that when their children came along it might not be unfeasible for her and Mr Holmes to move to London, so that she might be on hand to take charge of her grandchildren's upbringing.

For no good reason she could understand, Elspeth had experienced a very fierce and surprising shock of dislike for that suggestion. Into her mind had come mental images of her own childhood, of the farmyard and its inhabitants, of her mother's kitchen with its good smells and its untidy bustle, of laughter and sunshine, of love and warmth, and she had known instinctively that she would never ever allow her prospective mother-in-law to bring up her own children.

Disturbing though these thoughts were she had managed to subdue them, chiding herself for being over-sentimental, reminding herself of how ill-equipped her own childhood had left her for the hard realities of life and people. And yet . . .

'Elspeth, you aren't listening to a word I'm saying. Really, I don't know what it is about your family, but they do seem to have the most unsettling effect on you. If it weren't for the fact that someone ought to check up on what this man is planning, I'd have serious doubts about the wisdom of your spending so much time in Cheshire. Both apartments need decorating. You could have made a start on the painting while you were off.'

Elspeth focused on him, wondering why she didn't feel more enthusiastic about his suggestion, why she felt an almost sneaking sense of relief that she was committed to going home.

For no reason that she could readily discern, over these last six months she had experienced more and more rebellious moments of startling clarity, during which she had had the unnerving sensation that her relationship with Peter, her life here in London, her work, her scrupulous retailoring of her personality, her appearance, even her thoughts, were not an escape from the old childish, trusting Elspeth and her naïve country ways, but a trap—a trap which was gradually but inexorably closing around her.

Which was totally ridiculous, and fostered, she was sure, in some odd and indefinable way by her parents. Not that they would be liable to make those oh, so casual, but nevertheless pointed remarks about Peter this time. At least, not after the first three days, and she suspected they would be far too excited about their holiday to even think of remarking on how odd it was that she should choose to marry such a man.

Elspeth had never quite dared ask what they meant. She preferred to assume that they were simply marvelling at her good fortune rather than criticising Peter.

At precisely one-thirty, Peter summoned the waiter and paid the bill. At the end of the month they would scrupulously divide up the total cost of their total outings for that month, to make sure that such costs had been shared equally between them.

And if just occasionally Elspeth wondered what it would be like if Peter suddenly lavished her with expensive flowers or bought her handmade chocolates, she told herself severely that she was not that kind of dependent, childish woman, who needed to be bought such treats by a man; that if she wanted flowers she could buy her own. But something inside her refused to be totally convinced, making her cross with herself for yearning for such outdated, meaningless gestures.

'Time to go,' Peter informed her, standing up.

He said exactly the same thing every time they lunched together. Previously she had always found his predictability soothing, reassuring—but for some reason today it grated on her. She wondered what it would feel like if Peter suddenly behaved like her father, and announced that he had booked them both a surprise holiday, that he was taking her away to somewhere she had always wanted to go. She told herself severely that he would never do anything so thoughtless, that he would realise that it would not be possible for her to drop everything to go to the other end of the world with him.

No, if—when she and Peter took a holiday together, it would be one that was meticulously planned and organised, which was just what she would want. She could think of nothing worse than being told that she had less than three weeks in which to prepare for a two-month trip abroad.

Of course her mother thrived on such announcements, throwing herself into them with enthusiasm and as much excitement as a small child. But she was not her mother... No. She had recognised, the day when she'd stood in the doorway to the staffroom of the bank listening to Sophy, that for the rest of her life she would have to protect her parents from people like that. That she must never again subject them to the kind of cruel mimicry employed by her supposed friend.

Just before they parted outside the restaurant, acting on some impulse she couldn't understand, she leaned towards Peter, inviting him to kiss her.

A look of shock crossed his face. He drew back from her immediately, glancing hurriedly over his shoulder as though to make sure no one had witnessed her lack of self-control. He cleared his throat, avoiding looking at her. He was embarrassed, she recognised, flushing hotly, and no wonder. What on earth had possessed her? She knew quite well that Peter hated public demonstrations of affection.

'Er—I'm afraid I shall be late in tonight—I'm seeing a client. I'll ring you at the weekend. When would be a good time?'

Still flushed and angry with herself, Elspeth made an automatic reply, and then, having exchanged slightly guarded smiles, they both went their separate ways.

What a stupid thing for her to have done! No wonder Peter had looked so put out. They simply weren't the sort of couple to indulge in that sort of thing. Really, she didn't know what had got into her...

It must be because she was feeling a little edgy about confronting Carter. She had no real fears that she would be able to handle the situation and ensure that he understood that she was well aware of what he was up to—thanks to Peter. Nevertheless— nevertheless, half of her wished rather weakly that Peter were going with her, that perhaps... Not to deal with Carter for her—no, of course not—but just to be there as a sort of back-up—or just to be there full stop, she realised suddenly and rather disconcertingly, as the traitorous thought slid into her mind that for Peter to have parted from her so unemotionally and casually did not really suggest that his feelings for her were particularly lover-like.

But how ridiculous. What did she expect? A passionate embrace in the middle of the street? Of course not. Their relationship wasn't like that. They were far too sensible for that kind of thing. Their relationship was built of mutual aims, mutual respect, mutual goals. Rather disconcertingly as she headed back to the bank she remembered her mother once telling her nostalgically that she had fallen in love with her father the moment she'd set eyes on him; that she had known he was the one for her when he had rushed out into the road to rescue a kitten from under the hooves of the milkman's pony, daring both the milkman's fury and the amusement of onlookers when he'd presented the rescued kitten to her with a courtly bow of his head and a whispered confession that he rather suspected he had split his jeans during his heroic dive to rescue the kitten, and would she please go and stand behind him so that he could get to his feet without completely losing his dignity.

To envisage Peter in such a situation was beyond the power of the most inventive type of imagination. Peter would have ignored the cat. He never liked getting involved in things which did not concern him. He would certainly never have bandied words with the milkman, and as for wearing old and worn jeans in danger of bursting their seams... A complete and utter impossibility—thank goodness. She would have been mortified in her mother's shoes, to be aware of being the cynosure of all eyes... She shuddered and closed her eyes. She and Peter were perfect for one another—perfect. She was a very lucky woman— very lucky indeed.

So why did she feel so... so on edge?

It was Carter's fault, of course. If he hadn't come back into their lives, inveigling his way into her parents' affections... She had disliked him even as a teenager, feeling intimidated by him. He had teased her, she remembered, making fun of her braced teeth and pulling at her plaits. She at fourteen had been mortified by his reaction to her, and had retaliated by whisking herself out of the room whenever he had walked into it, and refusing to address more than half a dozen words to him during his entire visit.

'Not like your ma and pa, are you, cuckoo?' he had tormented her, she recalled.

She had been hurt by that comment . . . hurt and confused, although she had not let him see it.

Well, this time it would be different. This time she was an adult with no need to feel intimidated. This time he would see how very different indeed she was from her foolish, too trusting parents.

CHAPTER TWO

NOT much further to go now. Only a handful of miles—thank goodness. There had been so many hold-ups on the motorway that the journey had taken rather longer than Elspeth had allowed for. It was still light—just, the sky overhead remarkably clear, the moon and stars just beginning to shine. Thank heaven it was June, with its long, light evenings. She hated driving in the dark, especially down the narrow, winding country lanes that surrounded her parents' home.

As she pulled up at a set of traffic-lights, another car pulled up alongside her.

It was the sensation of someone looking at her, willing her to turn her head, that made her react instinctively, glancing sideways at the occupant of the other car—and immediately, angrily wishing she hadn't been so foolish as its male driver grinned back at her.

Elspeth glared frigidly at him. These traffic-lights seemed to be taking forever to change, and she wasn't used to being grinned at in that overly familiar fashion, especially not by strange men— especially not by a very large, very brown strange man wearing a short-sleeved shirt that was open almost to his waist, and a pair of disreputable shorts which revealed a pair of heavily muscled and extremely brown thighs.

At his age he ought to be beyond the stage of making unwelcome advances to unknown women, she decided bitterly, firmly refusing to give in to the temptation to cast him a second look, just to make sure he knew exactly how angry she was at his familiarity. He must have been closer to thirty-five than fifteen, but then he was obviously a particular type of the male species whom she most disliked: conceited, over-muscled—and boasting of those muscles by his state of undress—and driving one of those eye-catching, sporty little cars with its soft top down, its paintwork a bright and vibrant red. Just the sort of car that drew attention to its driver. Just the sort of car Peter would never ever consider driving—thank goodness. The lights changed and she waited hesitantly, giving him time to pull away. His type always loved to be first off the mark, and she was not anxious to draw up at the next set of lights alongside him. Thank heaven, after that she would be turning off the Chester ring road and heading for her parents' home village.

But as she waited for the bright red car to move the traffic behind her signalled its impatience at her delay, and she realised that the red car had still not moved.

Feeling uncomfortable and unnerved, she put her own small car in gear, wincing a little as she under-estimated the amount of clutch and shot forward in an ungainly and thoroughly inexperienced manner, galling in the extreme to someone who prided herself on her sensible, safe handling of her car.

As she glanced automatically into her rear-view mirror, she saw to her horror that the reason the red car hadn't moved was that its driver was now signalling to pull into her lane right behind her, and that the traffic, caught off guard by her kangaroo-like leap forward, had allowed him to do so.

Indignation rose in her throat. How dared he? Did he honestly think she was the kind of woman to be impressed by that sort of idiotic behaviour? Hadn't he realised from the look she had given— that look of freezing disdain she had soon learned to hide her real feelings behind after that never-to-be-forgotten occasion when she had walked into the staff-room at the bank with her real emotions written all too clearly on her face? Did he actually think she would be *flattered* by his obvious pursuit of her?

Things like this simply did not happen in London, where the drivers were far too anxious to get to their destination to play these silly games. And she had never in her wildest imaginings believed that she would be involved in something so juvenile.

Well, he would soon get tired of showing off and pursuing her, once she had made it plain to him that she simply wasn't interested. And once she realised she was turning off at the next set of lights he would soon return to the main stream of traffic.

By rights a man of that age ought to have far more serious matters on his mind than pursuing unknown women. If she had been of a less strong disposition, nervous and easily frightened, she could almost have been panicked into having an accident by his pursuit of her.

Men like that were a danger to the other traffic. By rights she ought to report him to the police, she told herself in annoyance as a peep in her mirror showed her that he was still behind her.

At least he had some sense, she noticed reluctantly. He was keeping a good safe distance between them, not trying to crowd up behind her.

Just as she approached them the lights turned to red, and, on an impulse she couldn't entirely analyse, instead of indicating that she was turning right, she did nothing... Let him think she was going straight on. That way she would make sure that he didn't pursue this stupid game any further. Although she was determined not to look in her mirror, she found that she *was* doing so. Simply out of habit, she assured herself. All good drivers kept an eye on the traffic behind them.

He had pulled up right behind her, and as she glanced into her mirror she saw to her fury that he was actually daring to smile at her a second time. A smug, self-assured smile, which said that he was quite sure that his insulting behaviour would be admired and welcome. She had a good mind to get out of her car and give him a piece of her mind. Arrogant, conceited creature... Couldn't he *see* that she just was not the type of woman to be flattered by what he was doing? Surely her immaculate, shoulder-length, straight red hair with its sophisticated London sheen and elegance, her thoroughly city-groomed suit and blouse, her discreet make-up, which emphasised her golden eyes and which

was delicately balanced on the right side of seriousness, told him that she was a career woman,
and simply not interested in flirting with strange
men in bright red cars.

A cold glare into her mirror should reinforce that
message, *if* he was so bone-headed that he hadn't
already received it.

This time when the lights changed she was ready
for them; deftly turning the wheel and flicking the
indicator, she pulled out and away, giving the car
just a little more acceleration than she would normally have used, and discovering, as she turned into
the quiet B road that led eventually to the village,
that rather disconcertingly she was actually holding
her breath.

Odious man. His sort ought to be locked up. He
probably had a wife somewhere and a family. The
poor woman no doubt doted on him. She could
picture her now, a pretty, sad-eyed woman, with
two quiet, subdued little children, suffering already
from their father's outrageous behaviour. No doubt
he never took his wife anywhere but preferred to
flirt with other women, leaving his wife at home
with his children . . . He probably kept her short of
money as well, Elspeth thought with a scowl.
Otherwise how on earth could he afford to run a
small bright red car which had never been designed
for family use? Why, it hadn't even had a child-
seat in the back. That was how little he thought of
his family, that he didn't even make any provision
for their safety.

Carried away by her rising tide of anger on behalf
of this fictitious wife and children, it was several

minutes before she looked in her mirror again. Not because she had any doubts about doing so—of course not... It was simply that there was no reason. As her glance flicked upwards, she braked instinctively in outraged reaction at the sight of the now familiar red car on the road behind her.

He had actually dared to follow her! The nerve of the man. If the road hadn't been so narrow, she would have stopped where she was, leaving him no opportunity but to drive past. She hoped when he got home that his supper was burned and that his wife was justifiably furious with him.

It was ten miles to the village, nearer to fourteen if one took the narrow, meandering lane that only allowed for the single width of one car and which involved a dirty and very damp fording of a local river. The last time she had gone down that lane, Peter had been furious. There had been mud all over his newly polished car and, as he had virtuously pointed out to her, if he had not had the windows closed the inside of the car would have been wet and muddy as well.

Well, if the driver of the red car insisted on continuing his futile pursuit of her, she would teach him a lesson that might make him think twice about bothering another woman the way he was doing her. She'd like to see how he explained the state of his now pristine car to his wife.

Far too angry to be afraid, as soon as the turning down the lane appeared Elspeth turned sharply into it, gasping out loud in fury as she realised that her tormentor had followed her.

Ignoring the fact that she was driving much faster than was normal for her, and praying that she did not meet anything coming in the opposite direction, she gritted her teeth, and hoped unkindly that the river was full after the recent spring rains. Her own car, a sturdy Volvo, would have no problem at all with the ford, but his...his...bright red *plaything*... Savagely she decided that she hoped the river was high enough to bring the thing to a complete standstill.

The mental image of him standing in the ford, having to push his car to the nearest garage, brought her a good deal of satisfaction. She only felt piously sorry for his poor wife, who would no doubt receive the brunt of his bad temper. His kind of man always reacted with bad temper when thwarted. They were so obnoxious that it never occurred to them that their advances were not welcome, that all women did not find them instantly and irreversibly attractive. Look at him now—still daring to smile at her every time she looked in the mirror, although now she noticed his smile was turning to a frown.

Did he realise what lay ahead of them? She certainly hoped so, she decided viciously. It was certainly too late for him to turn round.

She saw the familiar sign for the ford and dropped down a gear in readiness for it. As she had known it would, her sturdy car splashed through without any problems.

Safely on the other side, she watched in glee as the red car followed suit. The ford, muddy from her passage through it, came much higher up the wheels of the red car than it had done her own, and as she had hoped the muddy, gritty water soon marked the pristine scarlet of the car's over-bright bodywork.

Serves him right, she decided grimly as she pulled away, heading for the village.

The lane ended a few miles short of the village, curving back on itself to meet the main road. As she emerged on to it, Elspeth saw the red car pull up behind her.

To her astonishment, just as she turned out on to the road the creature had the gall to flash her with his headlights. Astounded at his temerity, she missed her opportunity to pull out. She could see a heavy stream of traffic coming towards her and blocking her exit, and as she sat waiting for an opportunity to move she suddenly heard the unmistakable sound of a car door being slammed.

Looking into her mirror, she saw to her horror that the man was walking towards her. Heavens, he was huge. She had guessed he would be tall, but he was well over six feet—much taller than Peter, who was only four inches above her own five feet six. He was also broad, and the shirt he was wearing looked even more disreputable at close quarters than it had done at a distance. As he headed towards her, plainly intent on ignoring all her attempts to show him just how little his advances were welcome to her, Elspeth was so incensed that she forgot the cautious training of her adult years, forgot all the warnings constantly given by the papers and police against lone women stopping their cars and opening the doors to unknown men, forgot everything bar the anger boiling up inside her, and just as he reached her car she thrust open the door and got out, trembling with rage and indignation.

'I don't know *what* you think you're doing,' she told him, going straight into the attack. 'But if you think for one moment that I'm flattered by your idiotic and juvenile behaviour, then you're wrong. And if you imagine that by following me and trying to get my attention you're going to impress me, then think again. I've a good mind to report you to the police, but I suppose your poor wife has enough to put up with. Your behaviour must be embarrassing in the extreme for her *and* for your children, but I don't suppose you ever think of that, do you? Men like you never do. I don't suppose you ever give a thought for anything or anyone but yourself. If you want my real opinion of you, I think you're detestable—detestable and contemptible, and if you don't stop following me immediately I shall report you to the police.'

Having said her piece, Elspeth suddenly discovered that she was trembling, as much with a strange sort of exhilaration as with anger.

He was standing in front of her in a most threatening manner, and she wouldn't have been surprised if he hadn't reached out and taken hold of her. She could see the way he was clenching and unclenching his hands. No doubt it had upset him to discover how little she welcomed his pursuit of her. Well, it would do him good to realise that not every woman he chose to pursue was going to fall at his feet in gratitude and admiration. Even so, justified though her anger was she had perhaps been rather foolish. They *were* virtually alone, and he was a very strong and now very angry man. A tiny thrill of sensation ran through her as she realised that if he did choose to take hold of her and, for instance, actually dared to kiss her, there was very little she could do to stop him. Of course, *if* he did she would make it immediately clear to him just what she thought of such disgraceful behaviour. She would remind him that he had a wife and family. Shocked by the direction of her own thoughts, Elspeth suddenly realised that she was standing there practically inviting him to make some sort of attack on her, and that she ought to get straight back in her car and drive off before he realised it as well.

As she did so, he took a step towards her, and said something she couldn't quite hear as a huge lorry thundered past, but she was pleased to note that when she eventually managed to pull out into the traffic he turned in the opposite direction. No doubt he had quickly realised his mistake. Well, she was glad of it. Perhaps in future he would think twice before subjecting some poor female to his arrogant and unwanted behaviour.

She stopped in the village at the local garage, which she knew would still be open, and which thankfully still had some milk for sale.

Despite all his efforts, Peter had still not managed to persuade her to drink her coffee black, and since her mother was still valiantly attempting to convince herself that both she and her father actually preferred the milk produced by their goats, if she,

Elspeth, wanted anything like a decent cup of coffee, she would have to provide her own milk.

Her stop at the garage delayed her longer than she had intended. The proprietor was a friend of her parents and wanted to chat, so that it was fifteen minutes before she could get away, by which time dusk had started to fall properly.

Never mind, she only had a very few miles to go, and there was virtually no traffic.

Secretly, if she was honest with herself, she still enjoyed coming home. There was something about Cheshire with its pretty countryside, so neat and clean, its fields speckled with black and white cows, its crops growing on land which had yielded harvests since before the Romans had landed and built Chester.

As she turned off the main road and into the narrow lane leading to her parents' home, security lights suddenly sprang into life at her approach.

Automatically slowing down, Elspeth stared at them in a mixture of surprise and approval. Ever since her parents had moved here she had been advising them to have these lights installed, reminding them severely of their potential vulnerability to thieves, but her father, while listening to her, had never seemed to take her advice to heart, and she had despaired of ever making her parents see the wisdom of her suggestion.

Now it seemed that she had been wrong. A further and equally pleasant surprise was the discovery that her mother's goats, which normally roamed the lane and the yard, providing a hazard for the unwary, were safely penned up in the paddock.

She could hear the dogs barking as she approached the yard, and the familiar feeling of anticipation mingled with anxiety gripped her stomach.

Anticipation because, no matter how much she might dislike it, there was still a part of her that missed this country environment in which she had grown up, and which reacted to her return to it with an almost heady sense of release; and anxiety because invariably she arrived home to discover that her parents had got themselves involved in one or other of the potentially dangerous situations they seemed to be irresistibly attracted to. Like children to water, she reflected in affectionate exasperation as she turned into the yard and neatly parked her car next to the mud-spattered red car, which must be the new one her mother had told her she was buying.

The mud-spattered red car!

Elspeth froze in her seat and stared at it in a mixture of dismay and disbelief. It *couldn't* be the same car—of course it couldn't. It was just a coincidence...and besides, this one had its hood up—and besides, how on earth could *he* have possibly known her destination?

Shakily she opened her door, reassuring herself that it was just coincidence, but as she did so a man rounded the corner of the house; a tall, broad-shouldered, dark-haired man who paused when he saw her and then looked at her.

It was the look that did it. She found she was literally grinding her teeth as she stood up, and she wished passionately that she was taller so that she could look directly at him instead of having to look up at him.

At close quarters the tanned face was not quite as suavely handsome as it had seemed. For a start the strong, high-bridged nose had been broken at some stage and was now slightly crooked, but in some odd way that imperfection seemed to add something elusively attractive to the man rather than detract from his appeal, lending his face a strength and character that a more perfect profile would have lacked.

As she stared at him, Elspeth even caught herself wishing almost wistfully that it weren't quite so dark so that she could see what colour his eyes were. What did it matter what colour they were? she chastised herself furiously. What *did* matter was that he had no right to be here—none at all—and if he thought for one moment she was going to be flattered by his presence...

Quickly, before she could weaken completely and give in to the totally unfamiliar foolishness that seemed to have caught hold of her, she told him as much, delivering the words in the sharp, crisp tones of the modern woman she considered herself to be; a woman who knew exactly how to deal with his sort of man and who lost no time in doing so, making it abundantly clear to him exactly what she thought of his behaviour.

It was only when she stopped to draw breath that she realised indignantly that neither of her parents had appeared to rescue her from him and that, instead of looking thoroughly chastised by her justifiable denunciation, he was instead watching her with a mixture of mockery and disdain.

'I hate to stop you in mid-flood,' he told her while she gulped in air. 'I applaud your performance, by the way. Your parents never said you were into amateur dramatics. A bit over the top, perhaps.'

Elspeth was still staring at him. '*My* parents?' she demanded, confused. 'You *know* them?'

'Yes. In fact... Look, why don't we go inside so that we can talk properly?'

Go inside? Talk properly? Elspeth looked wildly at him... Where *were* her parents? Why didn't they come and rescue her from this madman?

'Go inside...' she stuttered, stupefied that he should actually think she was willing to go anywhere with him.

'Mm. I've just about finished out here. I was going to wash down your mother's car, but I suppose that can wait.'

Her *mother's* car. She looked from him to the mud-spattered vehicle. 'That... that belongs to my mother?'

'Mm. She was going to buy a small hatchback, but she saw this in the showroom and fell in love with it. She said you'd be horrified and probably give her a long lecture.'

Suddenly another emotion was added to her confusion. This one was sharp and painful—desolation mingling with a sense of betrayal that her mother should discuss her with this... this stranger.

Immediately another and potentially scorchingly humiliating thought struck her, and she asked huskily, 'When you followed—er—saw me on the road, did you *know* who I was?'

She was praying that he wouldn't answer in the affirmative, and when she saw him nod his head she felt quite sick.

'Oh, yes. I recognised you immediately. You haven't really changed. Of course I was expecting you. Stupid of me, I suppose, but I'd expected you to recognise me too and when you didn't...'

He rubbed his hand along his jawline, and suddenly, and far too late, she did.

'You're Carter!'

Impossible not to keep either the shock or the chagrin out of her voice, and she realised as he looked down at her that the smile had gone out of his eyes.

'Yes,' he agreed curtly, 'and now that we've established that fact, perhaps we can go inside. I've had a long and tiring day, not made any better by a half-hysterical woman accusing me virtually of attempting to abduct her, not to mention my crimes against the wife and family I do not happen to have.'

As Elspeth stared towards the house, its silence suddenly made her suspicious. '*Where* are my parents?' she demanded, frowning at him.

'That's what I wanted to tell you. They decided to leave a few days earlier and spend some time with some old friends en route for Southampton. They left this morning—said to give you their love and to tell you you aren't to worry about a thing.

I promised them I'd be on hand when you arrived to explain everything. That's why I was hoping to stop you earlier—I was on my way to drive over to Knutsford with some provisions for a restaurant we supply there, but in the circumstances...'

Several things struck Elspeth at once. The first and most immediate was that she had made an utter and complete fool of herself and that, far from following her for the kind of nefarious and sexual purpose she had assumed, Carter was patently oblivious to her as a woman; the second was that betraying and very worrying 'we'. Had her foolish, too trusting parents already been tricked out of what was rightfully theirs?

Wishing desperately that they *had* waited until she arrived, she ignored Carter, turning her back on him and heading for the kitchen door.

To discover that it was not unlocked surprised her, and, while she was still staring at it in baffled fury, Carter stepped in front of her and inserted a key into the lock, deftly turning it and opening the door for her.

'A small precaution I've persuaded your parents to take. They're far too trusting.'

'Yes, they are, aren't they?' Elspeth agreed through gritted teeth. Why was it that this man was making her feel an outsider, an interloper, a stranger almost in her own home, frustrating and obstructing her at every turn she took?

Suddenly her head started to ache. She felt dirty and tired, and she longed almost ridiculously to see her mother come bustling towards her, soothing her with the promise of a cup of tea and some of her home-made bread. Silly tears of anger and weakness clouded her eyes.

Fiercely she dashed them away. Heavens, she hadn't cried since...since that episode in the bank's staff-room, and she certainly wasn't going to do so now, in front of this horrible, horrible man.

Abruptly moving past him, she headed for the door and the stairs, pausing only when she had opened it to say frostily to him, 'Well, it was thoughtful of you to be here to welcome me and tell me that my parents have left, Carter, but now if you'll excuse me I'm tired and rather grubby. I think I'll go straight upstairs and get ready for bed.'

Not waiting to see how he had taken her dismissal, she went upstairs. All she wanted was for him to take himself off to wherever it was he was living. Tomorrow would be soon enough to try to come to terms with the enormity of her own idiocy. All right, so she had made a mistake—a natural one surely in the circumstances. He was lucky she hadn't reported him to the police, hounding her like that. She bit her lip, wishing she wasn't able to imagine the scene at the police station had she done so. Carter she was sure would have relished revealing his identity, making her look a complete fool.

Of course he must have *known* she wouldn't recognise him. Why, it was over ten yeras since she had last seen him. Then he had had that thick, bushy beard and that wild, unkempt hair which had made him look unapproachable and rather dangerous.

He was still dangerous, to her parents anyway—but he was soon going to discover that *she* was a very different proposition, that she could see exactly what he was up to. Thank goodness Peter had had the wisdom to point out to her just what his motives might be.

Mingled with her exhaustion and her anger was another emotion, a sharp, dangerous emotion that hurt and ached, an emotion that made some secret place deep inside her heart feel sore and tender, and all because she had seen the amusement in his eyes when he'd informed her just why he had been following her, and she had known how much pleasure it had given him to refute her accusations. If he had said the words out aloud he couldn't have made it plainer just how little possibility there was of his finding her attractive or desirable.

Quite why that should hurt she had no idea—nor did she want to know.

She pushed open the door to the spare room. The house had four bedrooms, but as yet her parents had only got round to furnishing two of them. As it opened and she switched on the light, she stared at the room in confusion.

A man's jacket hung on the back of the desk chair, a pair of trainers on the floor beside it. There were papers scattered on the desk, and other articles of clothing on the bed . . . male clothing.

'I'm sorry, I should have warned you,' Carter's voice came from behind her. 'Your parents asked me to move in while they're away to keep an eye on things. Your mother said that you'd probably prefer to use their room, since it has its own bathroom.'

'You're staying *here*?' She couldn't believe it. It was all some horrid joke.

'That's right.'

'But there's no need. *I'm* here—I mean, that's why I'm here, so that I can take charge—care of things.'

'Your mother seemed to think you needed a holiday. I think she was concerned that it might be too much for you, and, since your folks have been good enough to offer me their spare room, until I find somewhere of my own, offering to take charge—care of things for them while they're away seemed the least I could do.'

She couldn't believe it. She *wouldn't* believe it.

Ignoring the man standing almost immediately behind her, Elspeth turned on her heel and with as much dignity as she could muster walked blindly into her parents' bedroom.

How *could* they have done this to her—and without saying a word? They must have known how she would feel.

She shuddered, trying to take a deep, steadying gulp of air. It would have been bad enough if she had simply arrived to find Carter already here, but to have discovered that he was a man she'd thought was pursuing her for a completely different kind of motive than he actually had been, was so deeply humiliating for her that even now the knowledge of her own folly was scorching her skin a dark and very hot red.

And Carter had enjoyed her embarrassment, just as he had enjoyed telling her that her parents obviously did not trust her enough to leave her in sole charge. Oh, he might pretend it was out of concern for her, but she knew better . . . and so did he. She discovered that she was grinding her teeth again, a wild and bitter fury overtaking her.

Well, he might be laughing now, but he would soon discover that she had his measure.

First thing in the morning, once she had had a good night's sleep and felt more like herself, she was going to make sure that he left. The simple reminder that she was virtually an engaged woman and he a single man should surely be enough to make him aware of the impropriety of their both sleeping under the same roof, even if her foolish, unrealistic parents had not done so.

And then, once she had got him out of the house, she would make sure that whenever he came to the smallholding she watched everything he did. He might think it was going to be easy, cheating her parents, but she was going to show him otherwise.

On this satisfactory thought a huge yawn overtook her, reminding her that she was very, very tired, and that tomorrow she was going to need all her energy and guile.

She gave a faint sigh and smothered another yawn. She *was* tired. And then she remembered that her case was still in the car. The thought of coming face to face with Carter now, when she was still feeling so shocked and disorientated, made her stop halfway to the bedroom door.

For tonight she would borrow one of her mother's nightdresses; she knew her mother wouldn't mind, and after all it was the least she could do, having been a co-author to her present predicament. How could her parents have done this to her? They *must* have known—and to have left without telling her, without waiting to see her... The suspicion suddenly crossed her mind that they might have deliberately left ahead of her arrival in order to avoid her angry reaction to Carter's presence.

For some reason that brought a resurgence of that odd pain in her chest. Angry with herself for being so silly, she pulled open one of the drawers in the old-fashioned chest her mother had inherited from her own parents, and removed the nightdress she found at the top of the pile.

She and her mother were a similar height and shape, although her mother was a couple of sizes larger than Elspeth. In fact, her parents always remarked when they saw her that they thought she was too thin, and Elspeth had given up trying to explain to them that, in the high-pressure world of business, a slightly lean and hungry look added an extra sharpness to one's image. And besides, without the constant temptation of her mother's wonderful cooking, it was all too easy to fall into the habit of eating light, nutritious meals. Without someone to share a meal with, there was no temptation to linger at the table; sometimes she found herself remembering wistfully the meals of her childhood, especially breakfast, when her father would come from his early morning farm chores and the three of them would sit down together.

Her parents had never been the kind of couple with nothing to say to one another; despite their rural life they had a keen interest in everything going on in the world about them, and when she herself had received her offer of promotion with the bank they had been the first to encourage her to take it up, even though it had meant her moving away from home.

She had missed them desperately at first, and sometimes she was ashamed to admit that even now she woke up in the morning, confused by the direction of the light coming into her room, wondering why she wasn't in her familiar bedroom at the farm.

She prepared for bed in the pretty, but thoroughly practical bathroom which her mother had had designed by local craftsmen, admiring the solid-lined oak cupboards, and the skilful way in which every inch of space had been utilised.

Outside the window the security lights suddenly went on, and as she tensed she heard Carter calling to her father's dogs.

His voice floated up to her through the half-opened window. 'Come on, girls, let's go and check the greenhouses.'

She found she was still holding her breath as she 6listened to his footsteps dying away across the yard.

Why had this had to happen to her? *Why* had fate seen it necessary to lure her into making such an idiot of herself? Why in fact had fate seen fit to thrust Carter back into their lives, to be the source of so much anxiety and irritation?

Sighing, she climbed into her parents' old-fashioned high bed, with its feather bolster and pillows, welcoming the coolness of her mother's linen sheets with their faint scent of lavender.

Tomorrow she would deal with the problem of Carter. Tomorrow.

CHAPTER THREE

DISTASTEFULLY Elspeth studied the clothes she had discarded the previous evening, reflecting that when she had decided against braving Carter in order to get her case, she had not looked far enough forward.

She had heard him calling to the dogs ten minutes or so ago. In fact, shamefully it had been that sound which had wakened her. Normally an early riser, she had been shocked to discover it had been well gone seven.

But now, with Carter out of the way, it might be a strategic time to nip downstairs and retrieve her case. Then she could get dressed and confront him with her ultimatum that he must find himself some accommodation elsewhere. She was quite sure that once she had pointed out to him the impropriety of their both sharing the same roof in her parents' absence, he would have no alternative but to agree with her.

The early morning sun had warmed the flagstones of the yard, and Elspeth's toes curled in sensuous appreciation of that warmth as she darted from the kitchen door to her car, quickly tugging on the driver's handle, only to discover that it wouldn't open. The wretched thing was locked, she realised frustratedly. But by whom? She knew *she* had not locked it—on the contrary. She gnawed worriedly at her bottom lip, knowing how Peter would have reacted to that piece of folly. He was extremely security-conscious, so much so that sometimes she almost found it irritating.

She was just mulling over this recognition when she heard the excited yelps of the dogs. Turning round, she fended off their affectionate welcome, bending down to pet them both.

Peter did not approve of pets, especially not dogs . . . especially hairy, over-enthusiastic and slightly undisciplined dogs. Perhaps once they had children she might be able to persuade him to change his mind. She would hate her children to grow up without knowing the pleasure of having a pet.

She was just about to stand up when she realised that the dogs hadn't come into the yard alone. Her breath hissed out of her lungs as she saw Carter standing in front of her, looking down at her with an expression she couldn't interpret.

This morning he was dressed in worn jeans, tucked into wellingtons, and a faded denim shirt that seemed to have shrunk as well as faded from the way the buttons strained across his chest.

Suddenly, for no reason at all, she was acutely self-conscious of the fact that her eyes were just about on the same level as his hips and that his jeans, while not exactly skin-tight, were certainly old and soft enough to make her aware that he was a man in a way that she was never aware of Peter's body.

Angry with herself for her almost too predictable feminine reaction to the sight of such a totally male and physically strong body, she attempted to stand up, forgetting that one of the dogs was standing on the hem of her borrowed nightdress.

As a result the neckline of the nightdress, while possibly perfectly demure on someone of her mother's proportions, dipped alarmingly under the pressure she was exerting on it, revealing, as she realised when she looked down to see why she couldn't move, a good deal more of her body than she had anticipated.

It wasn't her fault that, while her legs, hips and waist were enviably slender, her breasts were un-expectedly, and to her, embarrassingly voluptuous. So much so that she normally deliberately chose blouses and sweaters large enough to merely hint discreetly at their curves; her office suits had neatly tailored, pencil-slim skirts, but she always teamed them with long-line, generously cut jackets. This nightdress though was not designed for such a function, and as she stood there, trapped by Bess's paws and her own stupidity, trembling with chagrin, she felt the slow burn of hot colour seeping up over her skin.

To make matters even worse, as she bent down to free her hem, one frilly shoulder of the recal-citrant and devious garment slipped down her arm, so that she looked for all the world like some seventeenth-century milkmaid, flaunting her body for the delectation of her master. A small shudder of horror gripped her; that she who was always so modest, so coolly protective where her sexuality was concerned, that she should be put in this kind of position... All she had wanted to do was to retrieve her suitcase.

She finally managed to eject Bess from her feet, and, while the dog gave her a pathetic, ingratiating look, she managed to stand up, clutching what was left of her dignity—along with the nightdress—firmly around her to demand bitterly, 'Did *you* lock my car?'

'Yes. I should have thought you'd have done it yourself,' came the reproving reply. 'After all, you live in London. You must be aware of the incidence of car thefts. Just because we don't live in a city, it doesn't mean we're safe from crime here.'

Elspeth stared at him. At another time she would have been very quick indeed to reject his allegations, but right now she had more important things on her mind. Like her clothes.

'Well, if you wouldn't mind giving me my keys,' she began acidly, but he ignored her, frowning slightly as he came towards her.

For a moment she actually thought he was going to touch her, and she shrank back against the car. She could smell the clean soap scent of his skin, her awareness of that scent an intimacy that made her mind recoil in shock at her body's weakness.

'I shouldn't stay out here too long,' he told her warningly. 'The sun can be surprisingly strong; you're very fair-skinned and, by the look of you, you're not used to exposure to strong sunlight.'

Briefly Elspeth was lost for words. What did he think she was? A child? She opened her mouth and told him freezingly, 'Thank you for your advice, but it really isn't necessary. For one thing, it isn't yet eight o'clock in the morning and the sun's hardly strong enough to burn me at this hour, and for another, when I came out here it was simply to retrieve my case from my car. If it weren't for the fact that *you* had seen fit to lock the car and remove my keys, I shouldn't be standing out here now. So if you would kindly tell me where they are...'

She was conscious when she had finished speaking that her voice had risen several notes above its normal, even, calmly pitched tone, and that she was almost shaking with anger, while he—hateful, odious man—was simply standing staring at her with the sort of frown that made it plain that he thought she was over-reacting.

'Your case—I brought that in for you last night. It's in the hall. I realised when I saw it in your car, when I was doing my last round to check on the greenhouses, that you'd most likely need it this morning.'

A brief but telling look at her borrowed night-dress immediately made her uncomfortably aware of her nudity beneath it.

This was getting ridiculous, she told herself. She must stop over-reacting to the man in this totally inappropriate way. Just because, for half an hour or so yesterday, she had formed the totally incorrect impression that he had been trying to pursue her, that was no reason for her to be physically aware of him in a way that was so totally unfamiliar and so completely out of place that she felt burningly humiliated by it.

And that feeling was intensified by the realisation that, in her anxiety to retrieve her case from the car, she must have virtually walked past it in the hall without seeing it.

All her emotions, her humiliation, her anger, her feeling of helpless fury rolled into a hot, tight ball that lodged painfully in her chest, and for the first time in her adult life she experienced a strong desire not only to vocally tell her tormentor what she thought of him, but also to either throw something or burst into tears.

The knowledge that Peter, had he known how she was feeling, would have reacted with both horror and distaste did nothing to ease her feelings. Peter hated emotional displays of any kind.

Knowing that if she didn't put some distance between Carter and herself immediately she might well give in to the temptation to say or do something she knew she was bound to regret later, she turned on her heel and stalked furiously back to the house. Or at least she *tried* to stalk. It was rather difficult when wearing a borrowed nightgown that flapped round her bare feet, and with two dogs gambolling joyously at her ankles, and in the sudden and horrifying knowledge that, with the sun shining fully on her, the thin cotton of her mother's nightdress had more than likely become completely seethrough, thus affording Carter ample opportunity to see the outline of her naked body.

When she got inside she discovered that she was trembling, her hands balled into two tight fists, tension a physical band gripping her forehead. Why, when she could deal with any amount of difficult situations at work, was she suddenly falling apart, and all because of one impossible, scheming man?

In the kitchen, Jasper the parrot caught sight of her, and cackled hideously, screeching in a leering voice, 'Hold on to your knickers, girl!'

It was the last straw. Something seemed to snap inside her and, before she knew what she was doing, she was advancing on the parrot to say menacingly, 'For your information, I'm not wearing any, and if you don't keep quiet I'll wring that scrawny neck of yours, and bake you in a pie, you . . . you chauvinist.'

It was only when she heard stifled laughter behind her that she realised Carter had followed her in. As her head snapped round, two dark patches of colour staining her cheekbones, he turned his laughter into a hurried cough.

'Er—I wouldn't do that, you know. Your mother's very fond of Jasper.'

'Well, I'm not,' Elspeth gritted, glowering at both man and bird.

Having found her suitcase in the hall, she took it upstairs, showered and dressed, trying to restore herself to her normal confident, businesslike self by putting on a crisp cream shirt and a formal navy pin-striped suit. The suit was new, and Peter, when she had shown it to him, had remarked cautiously that he felt the skirt was a little on the short side. He had warned her against wearing it when they had visited his parents. His mother apparently considered any woman who wore a skirt that ended anywhere less than a good two inches below the knee to be unladylike in the extreme.

Elspeth remembered that she had been very irritated by Peter's comment, and had even been tempted to tell him that his mother's views were not written in tablets of stone. In fact, she had received a surprising number of compliments from her male colleagues when she'd first worn the suit. Not that she was flattered by such things. She left that kind of weakness to the male sex, who everyone knew were hopelessly vain. But even so, it would have been rather nice if Peter had remarked on how well the skirt suited her slim hips and legs, and even nicer if he had given those same legs the kind of long, lingering and very appreciative look she had inadvertently caught one of the young men at work giving her. Which was ridiculous, of course. She had long ago recognised that there was far more to a stable male-female relationship than mere physical admiration. She and Peter were two of a kind—everyone said so. So why did she suddenly find the thought of being two of a kind with Peter oddly depressing?

There was one thing for sure, and that was that Peter would not approve of her living under the same roof as Carter. Not that he would for one moment suspect her of doing anything wrong. No—of course not. That would be unthinkable. But Peter's mother certainly wouldn't approve. Periodically she came up to London, 'surprise visits' made so she said on the spur of the moment, but Elspeth had the distinct impression that they were more in the nature of a trap designed to ensure that she and Peter were still living separately.

Peter's mother did not approve of couples living together before they were married. Men were weak in these matters, she had once told Elspeth. Invariably it was up to the woman to ensure that a man's respect for her was such that he would not even dream of asking her to move into his home.

Elspeth approved of respect existing between the sexes, but sometimes she reflected rebelliously that her idea of respect did not accord with Peter's mother's. Sometimes—dared she admit it—there were even moments when she actually wished that Peter would suggest that they spend the night together.

That these wild, rebellious thoughts always seemed to occur just after she had paid a visit to her parents and witnessed their still obvious happiness together often made her reflect that Peter was perhaps right when he claimed that her parents were a bad influence on her. She knew he strongly disapproved of their, to him, over-casual approach to life.

When she had suggested that it seemed to work for them as they were very happy together—one only had to listen to them, see them... to Elspeth it always seemed as though her parents' lives were full of warmth and laughter—Peter rarely laughed, and nor, she realised, did she—Peter had been so affronted that she should argue with him that she had dropped the subject.

Reminding herself that it was Carter about whom she should be thinking and not Peter, she blew her hair into its neat, stylish bob, applied her usual discreet make-up and almost-no-colour lipstick and then headed for the kitchen.

Outside the door, she paused and took a deep breath. Armoured now in all trappings of her business self, she would surely be able to wrest command of the situation from Carter, and make it plain to him that she was not going to tolerate his presence in the house. She was sorely tempted to tell him that her parents had made a mistake and that she could manage the smallholding without his help, but, almost scrupulously honest with herself, she was reluctant to do so. After all, what did she really know about running such a business? It was her parents' livelihood, and if anything should go wrong...

Taking another deep breath, she opened the kitchen door.

Carter was just pouring coffee into two mugs. He looked up as she walked in and said casually, 'Good, I was just going to come up and tell you that breakfast is ready.' He checked and frowned. 'I hadn't realised you were going out this morning.'

'Going out?' Elspeth glowered at him. 'I'm not going anywhere,' she told him aggressively, 'but you are.'

He put down the coffee-jug, and ignoring the last provocative piece of speech said incredulously, 'You aren't planning to wear that outfit here, are you? I should have thought jeans——'

'What I choose to wear has nothing whatsoever to do with you,' she told him crisply.

'All right, no need to lose your temper. Especially not before breakfast—it will ruin your digestion. Come and sit down. Everything's ready. Your mother told me how you like your porridge.'

Porridge? Elspeth's jaw dropped. 'I loathe porridge,' she told him grittily, 'and I never . . . ever eat breakfast.'

'Well, you should. Your mother's right, you are too thin. At least, parts of you are,' he added musingly, and humiliatingly, as she was tormented by a vivid and unwanted mental picture of just how much he must have seen of the voluptuous curves of her breasts out there in the yard, a hot wave of colour crawled betrayingly up over her body, spreading until even her face burned with the intensity of it.

'I want to talk to you,' she told him when she had recovered.

'Do you? Well, come and sit down, then. I want my breakfast, even if you don't want yours.'

He was holding out a chair for her, and rather than argue with him she sat down in it and watched in revulsion as he tucked into one of the two bowls of porridge on the table.

Why on earth had her mother told him she liked the stuff? She knew it revolted her. Why had her mother been discussing her at all?

'What was it you wanted to talk about?' he invited.

Adopting her most brisk and businesslike air, she told him, 'I want you to find somewhere else to live. At least while my parents are away. You must see the sort of gossip and speculation it will give rise to if we both stay here. I suppose my parents left in such a rush that it never occurred to them how potentially embarrassing your being here might be to me.'

'Embarrassing?' he checked her. 'How?'

Elspeth glared at him. Surely she didn't have to spell it out for him? '*You* are a single man ... *I* am an—a virtually engaged woman.'

'Oh, you mean your—"almost" fiancé might object. Doesn't he trust you, then?'

'Trust *me*? Of course he does,' Elspeth retorted, incensed. 'Peter knows I would never...'

'Never what?' Carter asked her helpfully, suddenly abandoning his porridge to look directly at her, so directly, in fact, that the amber stare of his eyes seemed to have an almost hypnotic effect on her, making her forget every word she had been about to say. They were gold, she recognised in bemusement, a pure, clear gold. Instead she broke into a flustered and almost incoherent flurry of words, which seemed to plunge her deeper and deeper into a morass of confused admissions and accusations.

'I see,' Carter said softly when she had finally stumbled into silence. 'It isn't that this "almost" fiancé of yours would imagine for one moment that living under the same roof as me might incline you into any kind of moral decline, but you are afraid that his parents wouldn't feel the same way. What kind of man is he?' he asked her almost gently. 'Whose opinion of you matters the most to him— his own or his mother's? Come to think of it,' he added, narrowing his eyes as he looked at her, 'why on earth are the two of you not actually engaged, or better still married? Believe me, if I'd found the woman I wanted to spend the rest of my life with, I wouldn't take the chance of her getting away from me by leaving her free to find someone else. In fact, I'd fill her life and her thoughts and her bed so completely that she wouldn't want to find someone else.'

Elspeth gaped at him. 'If you're suggesting that *I* want to find someone else,' she accused recklessly, 'then let me tell you that you're wrong. I'm perfectly content with Peter.'

'Content.' The dark eyebrows climbed steeply. 'Contentment, my dear Elspeth, is for old age, not youth. No wonder this "almost" fiancé of yours doesn't mind your taking off and leaving him for weeks on end. If contentment is the best way you can describe your relationship...'

'I suppose if you were almost engaged you wouldn't even let the poor girl go away without you,' Elspeth challenged back. 'If there's one thing I cannot stand it's possessive men.'

'Oh, I'm not possessive. When you're in a secure relationship founded on mutual love, you don't need to be. I was merely pointing out that, to the outside observer, your relationship seems to lack a little passion. Still, if you're content——'

'I am,' Elspeth retorted, suddenly realising how far she had been side-tracked off the main issue. 'However, it isn't my relationship with Peter I want to discuss. It's the fact that it's impossible for us both to live here under the same roof.'

She waited, while he drank some coffee and chewed a piece of toast—maddening creature, he was deliberately trying to irritate her. Her stomach suddenly rumbled, contradicting her statement that she wasn't hungry. Chagrined, she bit her lip. What was the matter with her anyway? She never normally ate breakfast. But then she never normally lost her temper, she never normally discussed her relationship with Peter with strangers, and she certainly never normally virtually exposed her completely nude body to unknown men.

When he had finished he studied her, and then said blandly, 'So you'll be going back to London, then?'

Her breath hissed out in outraged fury. 'No, I shall not,' she told him. '*You* are the one who will be leaving. You *must* see the impossibility of your staying on here.'

'No, quite frankly I don't,' he told her almost sharply, suddenly dropping his casual, almost careless attitude, and staring at her across the table in a way which was almost intimidating. 'And if you don't mind my saying so I think your objections are positively Victorian, not to say almost paranoid. You can hardly really suppose in this day and age, and given the fact that your parents know that the pair of us will be staying here, *and* that you're virtually engaged, that anyone, apart from dear Peter's mother, is going to give the fact that we're both staying here the slightest thought?'

'So you won't leave?' Elspeth asked him flatly.

'No. I promised your parents I'd keep an eye on things while they were away, and that's exactly what I intend to do. If you want to stay, then fine. If you don't...' As he shrugged powerful shoulders, it occurred to Elspeth that he might be deliberately trying to get her to leave, giving him a clear field to create whatever difficulties he wished for her parents' business.

'*I'm* not leaving,' she told him, tilting her chin and glaring at him.

The look he gave her was decidedly odd—almost triumphant in some way, as though she had reacted exactly as he wanted her to, and yet that was impossible . . . He couldn't *want* her to stay any more than she wanted him to do so.

'Good, I've got a couple of auctions to attend in the next two weeks and, while I could have arranged cover for myself, it will be much better if you're here to take over just in case I don't make it back for any of the evening watering or deliveries.'

His casual assumption that she would fall in with his plans and allow him to dictate what she did further inflamed her temper, but she decided that she wasn't going to allow him to provoke her. She was sure that he would enjoy doing so, no doubt hoping that she would take umbrage at his attitude and leave.

Instead she asked as casually as she could, 'These auctions—I take it they're for land and property locally? Mum said that you were hoping to set up a similar operation to theirs.'

'Yes, that's right. There's more than enough business for both of us.'

He seemed to be reading her mind, Elspeth reflected, but she suspected he was lying. There couldn't be that many local restaurants wanting organically grown produce.

'So it's agreed, then. We're both staying, and if you have any problems with Peter's mother you can always refer her to me. I promise I'll swear to her that you never so much as touched me, and that your behaviour was impeccable throughout your entire stay.'

Speechless with rage, Elspeth contented heself with turning her back on him and pretending she hadn't heard. It might amuse him to make fun of her, and of course he *would* find her attitude amusing. No doubt he thought nothing of going to bed with whatever woman took his fancy. He looked that type—the kind of man who could never understand the needs and motivations of her kind of woman. It was just as well she was immune to the attractions of the male physique and good looks. The fact that he was very virile and very handsome meant nothing to her; it was a person's nature that was important. Take Peter, for instance—he certainly wasn't handsome, nor as revoltingly male as Carter, but his personality, his nature, his love for her—— She stopped suddenly, realising uncomfortably that Peter's personality was sometimes overshadowed by his mother's upbringing, that his nature could on occasions be a little sharp and unfeeling, and as for loving her... Well, Peter believed that emotional and physical love between two people wcrc treacherous foundations on which to build a stable marriage. Even so...

Even so... what? she asked herself a little bleakly, unaware that Carter had got up until he announced, 'John should have arrived by now. I promised I'd give him a hand breaking up the soil on the paddock. If you fancy a walk later on we'll be there until lunchtime.'

With a casual nod, he walked over to the door and opened it, leaving her alone and feeling oddly forlorn.

CHAPTER FOUR

OF COURSE, she wasn't going to go down to the paddock, Elspeth assured herself firmly, half an hour later, her things unpacked, the breakfast dishes washed, her body suddenly and inexplicably filled with a restless energy that took her across the kitchen to stand in front of the window and then back again to the door.

There were plenty of things she could do to keep herself occupied up here at the house.

Such as?

She valiantly tried to ignore the tempting inner voice that whispered that outside the sun was shining and that it would do no harm to just quietly and quickly take a walk outside. After all, it made sense for her to discreetly check on what her parents' two part-time employees' routine was. She had no need to go too close to the paddock. And wasn't it about this time in the morning that her mother normally went out to open up the greenhouses when it was warm?

It struck her, as she stood frowning by the door, that she really had very little idea of what actually was involved in the physical running of her parents' small business. On her brief stays with them, she normally spent her time trying to help her father unravel the complications of their antiquated book-keeping system, and in coaxing him to replace it with a modern computer.

True, she did sometimes stroll through one of the greenhouses with her parents, and she certainly enjoyed the fruits of their labours when she sat down to a meal. She knew that her parents had recently invested in a series of polythene tunnels which would enable them to grow over a longer period, and that they were hoping that this year their profit would be large enough to warrant their taking out a bank loan for a new greenhouse, but of the actual day-to-day physical work of sowing, planting out and growing, she had very little knowledge at all.

Angrily she chewed hard on her bottom lip and then stopped, disgusted with herself for this reversion to such an infantile habit.

It was almost eleven o'clock. She couldn't spend the rest of the day virtually a prisoner inside, and all because she didn't want Carter to think that he had won and that he was in charge in her parents' absence.

Come to think of it, perhaps he was a good deal more clever than she had thought; perhaps he had deliberately suggested she go down to the paddock, knowing that to do so was to be sure that she remained well away from it. And she had fallen for it. Why, for all she knew, he could right at this very minute be poisoning her parents' land, be destroying it, or contaminating it with the very chemicals from which it was supposed to be free.

Suddenly impelled by new urgency, she hurried across to the back door and then hesitated. She had no wish to arouse Carter's suspicions, to make him aware that she and Peter realised that his motives in becoming so friendly with her parents might not be entirely altruistic.

Her glance fell on the kettle and she smiled.

Of course. If she were to take the two men a drink, under the guise of proffering an olive branch... She would have a much better chance of discovering just what Carter was up to if he no longer thought that she was hostile to him.

Berating herself for not having thought of this before, for perhaps having aroused his sense of self-preservation and caution, she started to make some fresh coffee.

Much as it went against the grain to allow any man, but especially one like Carter, to think that he had won and that she was prepared to be sub-servient and obedient to him, sometimes one had to use a little caution and diplomacy. After all, this wasn't something she was doing for her own sake, but for her parents. They had worked so hard to establish this small and potentially profitable business and they were so proud of their joint achievement. They would be desolated if they were to lose what they had built up. It was up to her as their daughter to make sure that that did not happen.

Peter had been quite right to alert her to the danger posed by Carter, and she quickly squashed the small and rather uncomfortably disconcerting feeling that, in pretending she was now prepared to be friendly to Carter, *her* behaviour was rather underhand. Elspeth had always prided herself on her honesty, and it rather irked her that she should now have to adopt a less than truthful manner.

Frowning over things, she found a large flask and filled it with coffee, and then, as though to compensate for that small *frisson* of guilt, she found the tin containing her mother's home-made scones and cut and buttered some.

Putting everything in one of her mother's baskets, she opened the back door, momentarily starting as the parrot shrieked unexpectedly, 'Mind how you go! Mind how you go!'

He had been so quiet since Carter had gone out that she had virtually forgotten his presence.

The age of her parents' house, its thick walls and small windows, ensured that its interior was kept dark and cool even on the hottest of sunny days, and Elspeth blinked as she walked out into the yard and the brilliant sunshine.

Only one of her father's dogs seemed to have accompanied Carter, the other as though by some mutual canine agreement apparently having decided to stay on guard, just inside the gate. With the habits and instincts of her breed, she was lying in the shade, just out of sight of anyone approaching the house. She turned and grinned at Elspeth, thumping her tail on the dusty ground as Elspeth spoke to her, reminding her endearingly of one of the wicked collies portrayed so cleverly in a Giles cartoon.

She was less than halfway across the yard when she realised she ought to have changed her clothes. Her suit skirt was far too tight for her to lengthen her stride to one comfortable for crossing even relatively flat open land. The heat of the sun made the jacket uncomfortably warm, and her smart, low-heeled shoes were certainly nowhere near as comfortable on a bumpy grass path as they were for city streets.

It was less than half a mile to the paddock; she had grown up on a farm and virtually as soon as she could stagger had been familiar with the countryside. Whenever she came home, she always packed her sensible walking shoes and a couple of pairs of well-worn jeans.

Her wellington boots were still in the rack beside the back door along with those of her parents—so why on earth was she behaving like an idiot and trying to gingerly pick her way along a narrow, overgrown path, in clothes that any fool would have known were completely unsuitable for such an occupation? *Any* fool—even one whose only acquaintanceship with the countryside came from looking at the ads in glossy magazines.

From here she could see the paddock, and the two men working in it could see her, which meant that she could not go back and get changed.

The trouble was that she had been so determined to check up on Carter that she had forgotten that mad impulse when she'd got up this morning to dress in something that would make it clear to him the type of woman she was. And, much as she longed to go back to the house and get changed, or even to remove the uncomfortable weight of her jacket, she stoically refused to give in to that need, firmly continuing on her set course, and trying to pretend that she felt completely at ease in her ridiculous and unsuitable clothes.

As she passed the greenhouses, she saw that all the windows had been opened, and that the beds outside alongside them were filled with a variety of young vegetables, all growing healthily and organically.

Her mother had told her on her last visit that she had been discreetly picking the brains of some of the village's elderly residents, and that she was keeping a note of all the gardening tips they had given her, including a list of the various home-made remedies for various pests and diseases likely to affect their produce.

The paddock was separated from the rest of the smallholding by a hawthorn hedge, its greenery now at this time of year liberally sprinkled with wild roses, and as she approached it Elspeth drew a faint sigh of relief. Her calves were aching, and the basket had suddenly grown rather heavy. She had turned her ankles more times than she cared to remember and she was only thankful that it was dry underfoot.

And then she saw the stile, and frowned at it. Surely the last time she had come home there had been a gate here into the paddock?

The stile, although solidly constructed and perfectly safe, was not going to be easy to climb in her straight skirt—at least, not unless she hitched it up quite considerably. For a moment the indignity of having to climb the stile with her skirt somewhere up around the top of her thighs made her stop and bitterly curse herself under her breath.

She was feeling too hot and sticky, and thoroughly unlike her normal self; and certainly, she was sure, the image she must be presenting must be far from the one of cool elegance she normally showed to the world. A gust of hot wind teased her hair, blowing it on to her face so that she had to put down the basket to push it out of the way.

Still muttering under her breath, this time it was Carter she cursed and not herself. After all, it was *his* fault that she had come out here like this, that she had walked down that uneven path in these totally unsuitable shoes, that she was feeling so hot and irritable——

'Need a hand to get over the stile?'

She was so engrossed in her angry thoughts that she hadn't even heard Carter approach.

With the sun in her eyes, it was difficult to focus on him where he stood at the top of the stile, casually pulling on his shirt, although she could still see where his chest was streaked with sweat and what looked like soil. His hair was ruffled by the same hot wind that had tormented hers, but at least he was properly dressed both for his occupation and habitat. While she... Never could she remember feeling at such a disadvantage to any man. And it was especially galling that it should be with this one that she should be making such an idiot of herself.

Carefully shielding her eyes, she prepared to refuse his offer, looking suspiciously into his face for the amusement she knew must be there. After all, in his shoes, she doubted that she would have been able to refrain from having a good laugh at his expense, but to her surprise he was simply watching her with what looked like genuine concern, as though he actually had virtually walked the width of the field simply because he wanted to help her.

As she contemplated this fact, the strangest sensation assailed her. Elspeth was not used to men wanting to help her, to cosset and protect her. She had always told herself that those old-fashioned notions of what had once been considered to be good manners went hand in hand with a paternalistic attitude that had kept her sex in emotional and financial chains for far too long, and yet, as Carter finished fastening his shirt and came down towards her, she had an unwanted and rather shocking bleak awareness of the fact that Peter would never in a thousand years have done what Carter was doing. That Peter would have quite casually and calmly left her to struggle on her own without even thinking that she might need the strength to lean on.

Had it been his *mother* who was crossing the stile, though...

Unaware of how huge and shadowed her eyes had become, she stiffened when Carter asked quietly, 'Are you all right, Elspeth? It's a hot day, and although I'm delighted that you've decided to come down...'

He was going to make some comment about the unsuitability of her clothes, she knew it, Elspeth thought, her whole body tensing as she prepared to reject whatever it was he was going to say, but instead, apparently oblivious to her tension, he simply went on calmly, 'You shouldn't have gone to the trouble of lugging that heavy basket down here.'

'I thought you might both like some coffee,' she told him gruffly, too grateful to him for not mentioning her clothes to prevaricate.

'That was very thoughtful of you. Here, let me help you over the stile. No, you put the basket down. I'll take care of that.'

The heat must have had more of an effect on her than she had realised, Elspeth thought dizzily as she weakly put down the basket and allowed Carter to come so close to her that she could actually smell the hot male scent of his skin.

Such an unexpected and intimate awareness of him as a man—earthy, sweaty, vigorous and somehow or other, in the most startling way, producing a shockingly erotic response within her own body, kept her standing as tense and still as a statue, so stunned by her own response to him that she had no intimation of what he intended to do, until he suddenly swung her up into his arms and advanced towards the stile.

She tried to protest, but the unexpected sensation of being off the ground, of being totally dependent on the physical strength of another human being made her feel so vulnerable that she clung instinctively to him, her protest that there was no need for him to carry her and that she could quite easily walk shockingly smothered against the bare flesh of his throat as he shifted her weight slightly so that he could mount the stile steps.

It seemed he had heard her, though, because he replied casually, 'It's easier this way. Saves you having to tussle with that skirt of yours—or even worse, damage one of your ankles.'

She stiffly tried to hold herself away from any contact with his body—an almost impossible task, when he was insisting on carrying her in such a way that she seemed to tilt into it in a manner that was quite shockingly intimate.

Her heartbeat seemed to have accelerated to at least one and a half times its normal beat; her chest, she suddenly discovered, seemed to have trouble expanding enough to allow her to breathe normally. She closed her eyes dizzily, telling herself that if she could just blot out the sight of Carter's body, so erotically filling her vision, these unwelcome sensations would no doubt disappear, but immediately she did so Carter stopped moving, causing her to open them again very quickly.

She told herself it was the unfamiliar vulnerability of her position that caused that odd ripple of sensation to shiver caressingly down her spine as she found herself looking directly into the watchful depths of his eyes.

'Are you all right?'

The words seemed to rumble from somewhere deep in his chest, so that she felt as well as heard them. Amber eyes should look cool and aloof, not—not warm...and—and concerned, she decided muzzily as she dragged her gaze away from them and tried to focus on something safer, but Carter had shifted her weight slightly and his forearm blocked her view.

Odd how she had never realised before how very virile a man's arms could be. Carter's were wired with hard muscle, covered in firm, tanned flesh and dark hair which shone silkily in the hot sun. As she stared at him, wondering why on earth her mouth had gone so dry, and why she should suddenly suffer a deeply embarrassing and totally unthinkable compulsion to reach out and run her forefinger lightly down the hard curve of that forearm, the hairs on it suddenly lifted, just as though she had actually given in to that compulsion and caressed him, just as though he had looked into her mind and seen laid bare there the confusion and shame of what she was feeling.

Shock made her turn her head as though in rejection of what she was thinking, her gaze momentarily locking with his. He was, she saw, looking at her sternly, a tiny frown quilting his forehead, his mouth suddenly hard with tension.

'You don't feel faint or anything, do you?' he asked her abruptly.

She had been so convinced he had known exactly what kind of effect he was having on her that it was several seconds before she realised he had totally misinterpreted her reactions. When she did, she seized gratefully on the excuse he had unwittingly offered her and said, 'No... No, I'm fine. If anyone's feeling faint it ought to be you. There was really no need to carry me over the stile, Carter, I was perfectly capable of climbing it for myself. In fact, to be honest with you I would have preferred to be allowed to do so. The days are gone when women found it flattering to be treated as helpless pieces of china,' she added for good measure, her voice almost tart, as he completed his task and swung her carefully to the floor.

Not for the world did she want to admit to herself how much she missed the warm contact of his flesh against hers; and she certainly did not miss that odd breathless sensation that had swept through her... nor that idiotic awareness of him as a man, that unseemly desire to actually reach out and touch him. What on earth could have possessed her?

Flushing guiltily as she remembered unwillingly all that she had felt, she bent her head and made a pretence of dusting down her suit.

She was behaving ridiculously. She had never reacted like that to the sight of Peter's arms. Reluctantly, she was forced to admit that poor Peter physically was nowhere near in Carter's class. His body, while not precisely puny, was quite obviously that of a man who worked with his brain rather than his body. Peter burned in the sun, and for that reason never exposed himself to it. From what she could remember of the odd times she had seen him wearing a short-sleeved shirt, his arms were pale, almost hairless. Certainly they had never aroused in her the shockingly indecorous sensations that she had experienced just now—thank goodness. One thing she did know was that Peter would have been as horrified as she was herself if they had done so. Her reaction to Carter had been so... so primitive, so... so shockingly intense, so... so out of character, she thought helplessly, as she waited for him to retrieve the basket and rejoin her.

When he did so he was looking rather grim, she noticed, and, forcing herself to remember exactly why she had come out here, she told herself that he was no doubt surprised and not very pleased to see her.

She saw that John was using a rotavator to break up the soil, and while she watched, desperately focusing on the other man in an attempt to appear totally oblivious to Carter's presence, she forced herself to concentrate on the reality of what he was doing here.

No doubt that small piece of pseudo-gentlemanly by-play over the stile had simply been a means of getting under her guard, of putting her off the scent, and she—poor fool—had reacted to it as though she were sixteen years old and never been held in a man's arms before—never been kissed.

Kissed... Suddenly, traitorously, her thoughts rioted out of control, as she wondered what it would have been like if Carter *had* kissed her; if, when he had looked into her eyes then when he'd been standing on the stile, instead of looking away he had lowered his mouth to hers.

She discovered that her mouth had gone dry at the thought, that a nervy tension was gripping her stomach, and that inexplicably her lips were tingling slightly. She ran her tongue over them in nervous exploration as though she was terrified that, by some osmosis, she would discover an alien male taste clinging to them.

'Look, are you sure you're all right? This sun *is* very hot.'

Instead of being grateful that he had mistaken her reactions, Elspeth discovered that she was actually quite cross. 'I'm perfectly fine,' she snapped back at him. 'And as for the heat, this is my *home*, Carter. I might live in London now, but I've spent all my growing years here in Cheshire—under the heat of its sun,' she added sarcastically, and then before he could say anything she asked, 'What is John doing?'

'He's preparing the ground for sowing. Your mother wants to try producing more soft fruits; one of the restaurants she supplies specialises in a range of soft fruit desserts and they're very interested in anything she can grow here organically. We're having trouble with the rotavator though. We could do with one with a bit more power.'

As he spoke, almost as though it had heard him, the machine suddenly coughed and spluttered to a halt.

'Excuse me. I'd better go over and give John a hand.'

Watching as he broke into an easy spring, Elspeth blinked once or twice in the strong sunlight. She did feel rather light-headed, she discovered— perhaps that was the reason she had reacted so oddly to him. Much as she hated to admit that he might have been right, that the sun might be too strong for her, it was a relief to discover that there might after all be a perfectly mundane reason for her odd reaction to him.

After all, one read about people going mad when they were exposed to too much strong sun.

That, she reminded herself wryly, was in the desert, not in deepest Cheshire. Still, she clung to the comfort of the explanation Carter had unwittingly offered her, and it was true that she did feel extremely uncomfortable and hot in her suit. She shrugged off the jacket and set out doggedly across the field to where the two men were kneeling over the silent rotavator.

It seemed unlikely that Carter could do anything to sabotage her parents' work here in an uncultivated paddock, but it would do no harm just to hang around for a little while and watch what was going on.

Not for the world did she want to admit that as yet the thought of walking back to the house in her tight skirt, her hot, sticky tights and now her uncomfortably tight shoes was not an appealing one, but, after fifteen minutes of standing in aimless silence while the men worked steadily on trying to repair their piece of machinery, common sense told her that for the moment at least her parents' business was at no risk.

Besides, if she stayed much longer Carter might get completely the wrong impression and start to suspect that it was him she had come to see and not the paddock. Which was ridiculous, of course. Nothing could be further from the truth, but just to be on the safe side . . .

Giving the two men a cool smile, she broke into their conversation and explained that she was going back to the house.

'I'm sorry about this,' Carter apologised, getting up off his haunches and wiping his dirty hands off on his jeans, 'but we really ought to make a push to get this done before the weather breaks. The farmers' weather forecast says there's a thunderstorm on the way for later in the week.'

A storm—Elspeth shivered. She had always hated storms, not so much because of the thunder—it was the lightning she dreaded. As a very small girl she had once witnessed lightning striking a tree, and the shock of that occurrence had remained with her, buried deeply in her psyche, so that no matter how much she told herself that there was no need for her almost irrational fear, it was something she had never been able to banish.

Carter frowned as he saw her shiver, but before he could say anything Elspeth started to walk quickly away.

Not for the world did she want him to think she wanted to linger, to stay in his company. There were any number of things she could do up at the house, starting with getting to grips with her father's accounts.

'The stile!' she heard Carter calling after her, but she shook her head, indicating the gate at the opposite end of the field, and called back,

'It's all right! I'll use the gate.'

She would have a longer walk that way, but the last thing she wanted was the experience of being held in Carter's arms a second time, of feeling that irrational and far too intense awareness of him again... Wasn't it?

CHAPTER FIVE

To Elspeth's chagrin, she discovered once she was clear of the paddock that she had the beginnings of a stitch in her side. She had always considered herself pretty fit, and privately was inclined to be a little scornful of those of her colleagues who countered the excesses of their lifestyle by strenuous work-outs in fashionable gyms.

When she came home she unfailingly took the opportunity of indulging in a long, therapeutic walk, but not normally clad in a formal business suit and city pumps, she acknowledged to herself. Crossly she blamed Carter for this particular piece of folly, and therefore it followed that the pain in her side was his fault as well.

Why had her parents been so foolish as to invite him into their home? They were so naïve at times, so in need of protection. Thank goodness Peter had been so quick to suspect what Carter might be up to.

Automatically she left the rutted lane to follow an overgrown path that led back to the house. It skirted a small coppice and then ran alongside a pretty stream. The soft gurgle of the water tempted her to stop and stare into one of its shallow pools. As a child she had loved going with her father, when he could spare the time, to look for tiddlers, and for some reason now the old temptation came over her. The water beckoned, exercising its ancient fascination. It looked so tempting and cool, and her poor feet were so hot and sore. Behind her, beyond the hedge which separated the paddock from where she was, she could hear the staccato sound of the rotavator, proof that the men were back at work. There was no one to see her if she gave in to that temptation and removed her skirt, tights and shoes.

Wriggling her toes, she sighed in the blissful pleasure of being free of her constricting and totally unsuitable garments. If her silk shirt looked rather at odds with the ragamuffin, slender length of her bare legs, well, there was no one to see her. Unexpectedly, a tiny impish smile dimpled her mouth as she contemplated Peter's reaction to what she was doing. He would have been horrified, and with good reason, she scolded herself, but she still made no attempt to get dressed, instead carefully stepping down into the water, shivering in delicious pleasure as she felt its coldness against her skin, and the smoothness of the pool's pebbled bottom beneath her feet. As she waded carefully into the pool, she felt the familiar and intoxicating pleasure she had known as a child. Pausing, she tried to remember how long it was since she had last done something like this.

When she was twelve, perhaps. After that she seemed to remember she had begin to consider herself too grown up for such childish pleasures.

She sighed again, automatically perching on a large, dry boulder, her chin sunk on one hand as she looked down at the clear water, as though expecting to see there a reflection of her childhood self.

For a moment, contemplating the past, she had been aware of a faint sense of aloneness, of melancholy, almost—and yet why? She had everything in life that every intelligent woman was supposed to want: a fulfilling career, a good circle of friends, all of whom like herself had high-powered careers, which meant that their friendships were something which invariably had to take a back seat, a relationship with a man who also understood the demands of her career, just as she understood those of his, a future planned along meticulous and orderly lines—so why did she suddenly feel as though she was not getting the optimum satisfaction out of life? Why had she suddenly started looking around her, and seeing in the life she and Peter had chosen for themselves a certain lack of something—something she could not actually define, but which seemed to be epitomised by the sheer joy and enthusiasm which overflowed from her parents' lives? They had their traumas, their bad times and troubles, but they were so happy, so ready to take the moment and its transient joy and appreciate it. Sometimes when she was with them she felt as though they were the children and she the adult.

Absently she reached across to the bank and pulled out one of the tall, waving grasses, chewing on it consideringly.

It was only when she came home that she started thinking like this. Cheshire had a very disruptive effect on her mind. Perhaps because in London she didn't have time to dwell on things which might be better not dwelt upon. Certainly she did not have time to sit on rocks dangling her feet in six inches of freezing cold water, clad only in her underwear and a very expensive silk shirt. The very thought of Peter's reaction if she ever evinced any desire to do so brought a wry smile to her lips. It lurked in the depths of her eyes, reluctant and faintly unholy—an urchin's grin, all secret knowledge and naughtiness—or at least that was how it struck the man watching her.

Elspeth hadn't seen Carter. She was still deeply engrossed in her own thoughts, still defiantly pushing away the one thing she knew she ought to be considering, ignoring it and then returning to probe carefully at its edges.

Now, here in this peaceful place, she should think calmly and logically about the insanity of her outrageous reaction to Carter. It had been a reaction out of time and character, she had no doubts about that; but she prided herself on her intelligence, and the mere fact that she *had* experienced such an overwhelming sensual awareness of him pointed unmistakably to the need for further exploration of certain shadowed and vague areas of her relationship with Peter. Why, for instance, had she never felt like that with him? Why had she been almost relieved when she'd first discovered that Peter did not, as he'd put it in his slightly pompous way, think it was a good idea for them to develop the more intimate side of their relationship until such time as they were both properly established in their careers?

She had accepted his decision so easily at the time, simply telling herself that while they were both under such career pressure neither of them had the time nor energy needed to devote to becoming lovers.

Why did she now suddenly feel that both she and Peter were hiding behind the convenience of that excuse? What new and irreversible knowledge had she gained so suddenly in those few brief seconds in Carter's arms to make her so fiercely convinced that there was something essential and basic missing from her relationship with Peter?

'You're looking very pensive.'

At the sound of Carter's voice she almost fell off her boulder, swinging round defensively and glaring at him as she saw him standing less than four yards away, watching her.

'What do *you* want?' she demanded, standing up, and then furiously wishing she hadn't as she saw the way his attention was drawn to her legs.

'I was concerned about you,' he told her calmly. 'You looked a bit shaky, and once we'd got the rotavator going I thought I'd better come after you to make sure you'd got back to the house safely.'

'I'm an adult, not a child,' she told him acerbically. 'And now, since you can see that I *am* all right, perhaps you'd be kind enough to go away and leave me alone.'

She saw that his face had creased into amused laughter as he listened to her. 'You know, you sound just like you did when you were a teenager. You told me to go away then too. You said that the farm was your home, and that you didn't want me there...'

Elspeth flushed crimson. Trust him to have remembered that incident. She remembered it too and knew quite well what had sparked it. She had just been at that very vulnerable age of changing from a child to a woman and back again, sometimes in the space of less than an hour, and she had seen in Carter's intrusion into their lives someone who was taking her father's precious spare time so that there was none left for her. And she had resented that bitterly.

'I was jealous of the time my father spent with you,' she told him flatly, refusing to lie to him.

'Yes, I know.'

Surely that couldn't really be compassion she could hear in his voice? She had made the admission more as a form of self-punishment than anything else, and to hear that soft almost tender note in his voice had startled her.

'I was having problems too. My father and I had been on our own for so long, I wasn't sure how I felt about his remarrying——'

Now she really was startled. 'But you were grown up,' she broke in.

'At barely twenty-two?' Carter asked her ruefully. 'I might have thought I was, but I was very immature in a good many ways. Being here with your folks helped me to get myself sorted out a little bit...helped me to put things in perspective. In fact, that would have been a perfect summer, if it hadn't been for one very cross and resentful young lady, who stood very much on her dignity against me.'

He was teasing her, trying to get under her guard, Elspeth warned herself, steeling her senses against the rueful tenderness of his words. 'I was following my instincts,' she told him coolly.

She was becoming increasingly conscious of the coldness of the water, and of the bareness of her legs. Carter was standing right beside her things and, much as she longed to demand that he go away, she knew it would be ridiculous and dangerous for her to protest about the intimacy of their situation.

Trying to appear careless and unconcerned, she paddled back to the bank, only to find she was as embarrassed and as flustered as her teenage self might have been when Carter remarked softly, 'Well, one thing certainly hasn't changed. You've still got the best legs I ever remember seeing.'

For a moment she was too stunned to say anything, to do anything, other than subdue the ridiculous flutter of pleasure that warmed her stomach, and try to combat its insidious effect by saying acidly, 'That is an extremely sexist remark, and one I do not appreciate. How would you like it if I were to make a similar comment about you—if I were to say, for instance, that I—that I found your arms very sexy?'

The moment she had uttered this challenge, she wished she had been more cautious. For a moment she thought he was going to burst out laughing, but instead he turned his head away from her, so that all she could see was the unexpected dark burn of anger along his cheekbones.

'You see?' she told him, trying to sound triumphant. '*You* don't like it. It makes you angry.'

'Angry?' he demanded vehemently. 'You think I'm *angry*?'

She could understand why he might try to deny it. No man liked being bested by a woman proving her point. 'Oh, you can try to pretend now that you aren't. I saw your face, remember, and you were angry...'

His mouth thinned and the look he gave her suddenly made her feel as though she were once again fourteen, a child in a world of adults.

'I don't know what kind of relationship you've got with this "almost" fiancé of yours,' he told her roughly, 'but it certainly hasn't taught you much about men. And the first and most important lesson you can ever learn is how to tell the difference between anger and arousal. I'll give you a head start. This is what happens when it's arousal.'

He moved so quickly she had no chance to escape. One moment she was still standing ankle-deep in the water, the next she was in his hands, pressed the length of his body as those same hands smoothed over what seemed like every inch of her skin from her shoulders to the tops of her thighs, stunning her so much by the sensations they aroused that she never even thought to move; could in fact only stand there, completely at the mercy of feelings she had never known might exist, blind, deaf and dumb to everything but the message Carter's touch was relaying to her as he held her against his body and brought his mouth down on hers.

As she realised what was about to happen some latent sense of self-preservation came to her rescue. She tried to turn her head away, but Carter was too quick for her, cupping her face with one hand while the other gripped her waist. How could it be that the pressure of a man's hand against her skin could at once be both so tender and so firm? Her movements stilled automatically as though he had spoken directly to her brain. Her lips actually parted in breathless anticipation of his kiss; even the water seemed to slow its flow so that the music it made lulled and hypnotised her.

There had never been a kiss quite like it . . . certainly not one she had ever experienced.

Peter's kisses were tepid, safe affairs, reinforcing her own belief that, as far as sex was concerned, she was one of those members of the human race whose appetite in that direction was slender rather than hearty. This self-admission had never particularly bothered her; after all, more and more City high-flyers, men as well as women, were now 'coming out', so to speak, and admitting that the stressful pressures of their careers left them not just short of time in which to make love, but short of desire as well.

It was the nineties' counter-revolution to the sixties, fuelled by the dread of AIDS, and until this moment in time she had never really paused to give her lack of any strong physical desire for Peter much thought, simply accepting it as a facet of a modern relationship. Theirs was a generation overdosing on high career achievement, burned out by stress and helplessly addicted to the narcotic of work.

Beneath the subtle alchemy of Carter's mouth, her own softened, her lips clinging, shaping themselves to the silent demands of his.

She had no thought of breaking away. No thought of doing anything other than hungrily absorbing this startling new pleasure that turned her mind weak and sent her blood singing dizzily along her veins.

There was no past, no future, no Peter...nothing to remind her of her suspicions over this man, only this elementary, singing pleasure to mystify and dazzle her, to lure her on to her own self-destruction.

The shock of Carter's suddenly wrenching himself away from her was a brutal reminder of reality. As she stood, dazed and disbelieving, unable to stop herself from pressing her fingers against her mouth, as if by doing so she could capture the feeling of his against it, she heard him curse under his breath.

'The rotavator's stopped again.' He still had his back to her. He was looking towards the paddock, but she knew humiliatingly that he didn't want to look at her. 'I'd better go and see what's happening before John comes in search of me.'

Not a word about what had happened. But after all what was there to say?

As she watched him walking away, absently noticing the smooth co-ordination of his body, achingly aware of a sense of tremendous loss and misery, she shivered coldly in the advance wave of a vast sea of guilt, confusion, humiliation and anger.

How could she have allowed him to kiss her like that? she berated herself as she quickly got dressed, pulling on her things with clumsy, stiff fingers, while her body trembled under the lash of her own destructive self-contempt. She wasn't a child. It had been up to her to bring a swift and firmly rejecting end to what had been no more than a very obvious piece of chauvinistic male by-play. Carter had wanted to torment her a little, and predictably had chosen a very obvious and male way of doing so. And she was largely to blame for that. If he hadn't found her paddling in the stream, half undressed, she doubted that it would even have crossed his mind to touch her. After all, he didn't desire her, not her—the person, the woman. He had simply been briefly aroused by her physical presence. There had been nothing remotely personal in that arousal—she might have been any woman. What she ought to have done was to have let him take his kiss, to have stood cool and remote beneath it, instead of which . . . Instead of which . . . She stood still staring into space, a fine shudder of self-loathing rippling through her as she remembered the way she had responded to him, offering him no resistance at all, and even worse . . . She trembled visibly as she remembered how her body had moulded itself to his, how her lips had softened and clung, how she had sighed and melted, and how, even if he had made no move to do so, had he chosen he might have caressed her far more intimately without her even thinking of stopping him.

Was it only this morning she had wondered what it would be like to be kissed by him? Well, now she knew, and she wished to God she did not have that knowledge, because she knew already, intuitively, irreversibly, that the memory of that one kiss would remain with her for the rest of her life.

And yet why—why should the touch of one man's lips affect her so powerfully? It wasn't even as though she liked Carter or admired him. It wasn't as though there was any kind of trust or respect between them.

There had been a moment before he'd kissed her when she had been given an unexpected glimpse into his past, when she had realised that the tough and very grown-up male she remembered had been nothing of the kind. With that knowledge had come a second's fleeting sadness that she had been too young to understand and know him better. Was *that* why she had responded to him, so shockingly?

It must be, she tried to comfort herself as she finished dressing and hurried back to the house. After all, there had to be some kind of explanation; the man was only human for heaven's sake and not some kind of sorcerer with the power to...to what? Make her desire him? Uncomfortably she recalled how peculiarly aware of him she had been well before he'd kissed her. It was just because he was so different from Peter, she reassured herself; because she herself was so unused to men who were so...so male. So what was she admitting? That she had turned into marshmallow in his arms simply because she was turned on by him physically?

Little as she liked to admit that she was capable of anything so out of character and extraordinary, it did seem to be the only feasible explanation. She firmly ignored the small voice that pointed out dulcetly to her that all through her teenage years she had been surrounded by well-muscled young men, and that she had never once felt anything like that shocking desire for them which she had just experienced with Carter.

It was a case of arrested development, she told herself tartly, and of course it meant nothing; absolutely nothing at all, and just to prove it she would telephone Peter when she got in and ask him if he could manage to tag an extra couple of days on to his weekend so that they could spend more time together. *That* would show Carter just how little that kiss had meant to her.

Heavens, from the way he had turned his back on her and been so obviously eager to escape, anyone would think that he was terrified she might try to turn that kiss into something far more important than it had actually been. Men were so vain—especially men like Carter. And besides, he had no right to go round kissing women like that, when it plainly meant nothing whatsoever to him. It would serve him right if she *did* allow him to believe that she was attracted to him. If it weren't for the fact that she had too much pride, too much self-respect to invite any further humiliation, it might almost have been worthwhile doing so, and watching him squirm as he tried to tell her that he didn't want her. And then of course there was Peter. Of course, as an almost engaged woman, she couldn't do anything so foolish. But that was what Carter had been banking on when he'd kissed her, she decided scornfully. Knowing that she was committed to another man, he had thought it safe to kiss her...

By the time she was actually back in the kitchen, she had managed to subdue the rebellious and disconcerting sensations she had experienced in Carter's arms to such an extent that she had almost convinced herself that she had never experienced them at all. Almost.

Sadly, when she went up to her borrowed bedroom to change into something more suitable, as she stood in her parents' bathroom stripping off her clothes she caught sight of her reflection in one of the wall mirrors. Her face was slightly flushed, her mouth surely a deeper red than usual, her hair windblown and softly tousled.

She paused, and then on an impulse she didn't want to name quickly removed her skirt, studying herself in the mirror as Carter must have seen her as she'd stood in the stream.

A small shudder of shock went through her as she recognised how provocative she must have appeared. Her silk shirt, so respectable when worn tucked into her skirt suit, somehow or other took on a decidedly wanton allure when it was all that she was wearing, and when furthermore it revealed the entire length of her legs virtually from the top of her thighs. Had the silk always clung so...so lovingly almost to the curves of her breasts, almost as though the fabric loved its contact with them? And *why* had she never noticed before how very far from demure the neat row of buttons that marched up to her throat actually was, almost

visibly enticing a man to slide them free and lay
bare the flesh they covered.

A sudden startling awareness that within a few
more seconds she would actually be mentally visualising a male hand caressing her flesh brought
her abruptly back to reality. It was Peter she had
been thinking of, of course, she assured herself
feverishly as she turned her back on the mirror and
quickly dressed. It had been the thought of seeing
him next weekend which had sparked off that
sudden spiral of heat inside her, that tiny aching,
yearning of her suddenly restless body.

This time when she dressed she took no chances,
firmly donning a pair of jeans and a workmanlike
cotton shirt.

It was only when she went downstairs to telephone Peter that she realised that she was going to
have to insist on Carter's finding somewhere else
to stay the weekend of Peter's visit. The house only
had two furnished bedrooms. She would deal with
that problem later, she told herself uncomfortably.
After all, it was no concern of Carter's whether or
not she and Peter shared the same bed, and there
was certainly no reason for her to feel awkward and
reluctant to let him know that they did not.

It took her several minutes to get through to
Peter, and, when she told him why she was ringing,
he seemed to hesitate before saying cautiously,
'Well, it should be possible, although I'd rather
promised Mother that I'd spend a couple of days
with them next month. She wants to clear out the
loft and I've promised her I'll lend a hand. How
are you coping?'

Quickly she explained about Carter, stumbling a little over her description of how astonished she had been to find him in residence and how unsuccessful had been her attempts to get him to leave. 'In the end I thought it might be easier to keep an eye on him and find out exactly what he's up to if I let him stay,' she added lamely.

'You mean he's actually staying there? Living in your parents' home unsupervised? Your parents really are totally irresponsible, Elspeth. It's just as well you *are* there to keep an eye on him.'

Wondering why on earth she should feel so irritated and angry that it was her parents' business Peter was concerned for and not her, Elspeth reminded herself that theirs was a relationship founded on mutual trust and that the last thing she would have wanted was Peter breathing fire and brimstone like a jealous lover, demanding to know what the hell she was doing living under the same roof as another man.

'So you'll let me know, then, about next weekend?' she asked him, sensing his anxiety to conclude their conversation.

'Yes, of course; and Elspeth... Next time perhaps you'd ring me in the evening at home. You know how I feel about personal calls at my chambers...'

Swallowing the small, rebellious spurt of resentment, Elspeth duly apologised and replaced the receiver. And then, for no reason she could think of, she said very fiercely and out aloud, 'Damn Carter.'

'Let's have a nice cup of tea.'

The sound of her mother's soothing, soft voice behind her made her spin round in astonishment, but the room was empty. Apart from Jasper the parrot, she realised as she caught sight of the bird staring devilishly at her.

'Good chap, Carter,' he told her, faithfully imitating her father's voice and causing her to say peevishly,

'No, he isn't. He's . . . he's a snake in the grass,' she told the parrot irately, but Jasper wasn't listening to her any more.

CHAPTER SIX

CARTER hadn't returned for any lunch, which didn't bother her in the least, Elspeth told herself firmly, as she made plans for how to spend her afternoon.

It was tempting to pick up the new paperback she had found in the sitting-room and spend the rest of the day sitting outside in her mother's pretty garden; after all, officially at least, she *was* on holiday.

With a start she realised how little thought she had actually given to her work. Normally whenever she was absent from the office she was itching to get back, suffering something approaching withdrawal symptoms, but this time Carter and his invidious behaviour had taken up so many of her thoughts that there hadn't been any room to spare for worrying about work.

And of course she wasn't going to idle away her time while she was here. Briskly she decided that she would spend the afternoon in her father's office sorting out his paperwork. Something she doubted he would thank her for, but her orderly, efficient mind could not bear to see the state in which he managed to reduce even the most simple accounting procedures.

Firmly resisting the temptation of the sunshine outside, she made herself a fresh cup of coffee and headed for the office.

Behind, Jasper was saying in her father's voice, 'Is there any tea going, love?' and then somehow or other producing the sound of someone pouring tea into a mug.

'Show-off,' she criticised under her breath as she opened the door into the office and stepped inside.

For a moment she thought she must have come into the wrong room. She stared at her father's desk, which was somehow smaller and less familiar without its normal burden of scattered papers filed haphazardly in a selection of cardboard boxes that meant nothing to anyone but him.

Behind the desk on the shelves that normally held untidy piles of out-of-date *Field* and *Horse and Hound* were a dozen or more neatly indexed filing boxes.

But most astounding of all, sitting squarely on the pristine neatness of her father's desk was a brand-new, up-to-date computer terminal complete with screen and printer.

Elspeth literally could not believe her eyes. She remembered the number of occasions on which she had virtually pleaded with her father to bring himself into the nineties with the purchase of such equipment.

How he had argued, prevaricated, claimed that he had no use for such new-fangled nonsense, and even when her mother had wryly informed her that it was his fear of the technicality of such equipment that was making him stick so rigidly to his determination not to get one, Elspeth had still not been able to convince him that he would master the technique of using it within weeks.

She had even offered to teach him herself, to set up a series of easy systems for him to use, and, when that failed, she had actually threatened to buy him the equipment and book him on to one of the many excellent computer familiarisation programmes run all over the country.

Still he had remained obdurate, stubbornly so, almost to the point where he had actually become annoyed with her. Which was totally unlike her gentle, mild-mannered father. So much so that she had reluctantly dropped the subject, even though nothing could convince her that with a little patience he would not soon have mastered the art, and that, as a result, the dreaded monthly chore of working on the accounts could have been reduced to a task of manageable proportions.

After all that she had been through, to see the untidiness of his office restructured into this model of modern technology neatness almost took her breath away. She blinked several times as though half believing that she might be hallucinating. To say that she was flabbergasted came nowhere near describing what she was feeling.

What on earth had happened to persuade her father to change his mind, and to have gone ahead and got the equipment without consulting her? Like a tiny maggot gnawing away at her initial delight that her father had at last seen sense was a brief flaring of chagrin that he had not consulted her. She dismissed it quickly as idiocy. Of course it didn't matter that he hadn't consulted her. What mattered was that he had finally done something about putting his bookwork in proper order.

She walked round the desk and studied the computer more closely, relieved to see that it was one of the most reliable models on the market; that in fact it was the very model she would have probably recommended herself.

She heard the back door open and turned around. Carter must be back. For some reason she suddenly felt extremely flustered and acutely uncomfortable. If anyone was feeling uncomfortable it ought to be him, she reminded herself grittily. *He* was the one who had instituted that kiss, not her.

But he wasn't the one who had allowed it to get out of control, who had encouraged and abetted it in getting out of control, she acknowledged guiltily.

She had a moment's cowardly temptation to close the study door and stay where she was, but it wasn't in her nature to run away from unpleasant situations, and so, squaring her shoulders, she walked quickly towards the kitchen.

After all, she was going to have to face him sooner or later, and she wasn't going to have him thinking that she had been affected by the kiss. No, her best plan of action was to behave as though it had never happened, to ignore the whole thing. And if he should mention it—should apologise, for instance—well, then she could simply say airily that she had forgotten the whole affair. All she had to do was to remind herself that she was committed to Peter and that Carter knew that fact.

As she walked into the kitchen she was stunned to hear her own voice saying almost desperately, 'But Peter, I need you.'

It was several seconds before she realised that the parrot had overheard her telephone conversation and was mimicking her.

Her colour high, she pushed open the kitchen door. Carter was just filling the kettle. He was frowning, she noticed.

'Did you manage to get the rotavating done?' she asked him, trying to sound casual and normal.

'Most of it. We had to knock off to come back and start the watering. Which reminds me, if you've got the time it might be an idea if you came and watched. It's too much for John or Simon to manage alone, and since I'm not going to be here for a couple of afternoons . . .'

'That would be fine,' she assured him, quite pleased with herself for managing to sound so businesslike and detached. That was the right way to behave, to pretend he was simply a very distant acquaintance with whom she had to be polite for form's sake, a stranger with whom she had been thrown into unwanted intimacy but who would soon be gone from her life.

'I was going to spend the afternoon sorting out Dad's accounts, but I see that he's taken my advice at last and bought himself a computer.'

It was a casual, throw-away remark, meant only to fill the yawning gap of dangerous silence which she felt threatening, but instantly Carter tensed, carefully turning his head away from her. For a moment she was completely puzzled, wondering what on earth it was she had said to warrant that watchful, fragile silence, and then she knew.

'It was you, wasn't it?' she demanded, abandoning discretion and caution. '*You* persuaded him to buy it. Oh, I might have known,' she added bitterly. 'It doesn't matter what I say to him. I'm only a daughter—a female. But let some fellow male come along, some member of his own sex, and suddenly it's all different.'

'Look, it wasn't like that. As a matter of fact your father remains as obdurately convinced that computers are an alien species as he's always been. Actually, it's your mother who uses the equipment. She's proved remarkably adept at doing so.' He gave a warm chuckle. 'She says it's doing wonders to help her with her cataloguing.'

'My mother!' Now Elspeth was astonished.

'Why so surprised?' She heard the faintly critical note in his voice. 'Your mother's a very intelligent woman.'

'Yes. Yes, I know she is,' Elspeth agreed, suddenly discovering that she would very much like to sit down. Her head was spinning with shock. Why had *she* never realised that her mother was interested in learning to operate a computer? Why had her mother never said anything to *her*? Why had she confided in Carter—a stranger? Was no member of her sex immune to him? she wondered savagely. What Machiavellian power did he possess to make women so vulnerable to him?

She had always considered that she and her parents—both her parents—were close, and yet here was this man, this stranger, telling her things about them that confounded that belief. Things like her parents' plans for expansion, her mother's skill with the computer... Why had she not been a privy to these things?

She pushed these questions aside, not wanting to dwell on them, not wanting to believe that her parents could have confided more readily in Carter than they had in her.

'These auctions,' she asked him abruptly. 'You never said exactly when they were to take place.'

'There's one tomorrow afternoon, and the other's next week.'

'Oh. And the land—is it local?'

'Fairly,' he told her non-committally, turning back to the boiling kettle.

'You *want* to live locally, then?' she pressed him, her suspicions freshly aroused. 'But surely if your venture isn't going to compete with my parents' it doesn't matter where you live?'

It was the closest she dared come to betraying her suspicions to him. A warning shot across his bows, she decided, not wanting to admit that the urge to fire it had somehow or other been caused by the knowledge that it was he who was responsible for that gleaming computer, that tidy office, that change in the familiar routine of her parents' lives which had taken place without her knowledge.

'Perhaps not, but it's always pleasant to live somewhere where one has friends, family. I like this part of the world. I always have done, and your folks have been good friends to me. Once I get my own place, I know I'm going to be relying heavily on their advice and support.'

And on *their* business? The words were on the tip of her tongue, but she suppressed them. It was one thing to subtly warn him that she wasn't like her parents, that *she* didn't trust him. It was quite another to openly accuse him. No, when she made her dénouement she wanted her parents to be there to witness it. How could he stand here in front of her in their home spouting about how fond of them he was, when he was planning to steal their livelihood? Indignation flashed momentarily in her eyes as she watched him.

'But you're a scientist,' she pointed out. '*You* don't have any experience of growing things. You've lived all over the world. Can you honestly believe you'll be happy to settle down in one small place?'

'I'm a biologist,' he corrected her mildly. 'And I've always been interested in the production of the food chain. A lot of people believe we've gone too far in interfering with nature, and in virtually manfuacturing our food with chemicals. There's an increasing demand for food which is untampered with.'

'And *you* want to produce it.'

'I'd certainly like to give it a try,' he agreed blandly, ignoring the cynical disbelief of her question. 'In the meantime, however, it's time I joined John and helped him with the watering. If you're ready...?'

Nodding brusqucly, Elspeth walked towards the door, and said pointedly, 'I'll wait down by the greenhouses for you, shall I?'

The way his mouth tightened sent a tiny *frisson* of sensation crawling down her spine, an awareness of excitement and danger—although how could anger be exciting? She had never found it so in the past.

As she closed the kitchen door behind her she heard the parrot saying conversationally, 'Nice chap, Carter.'

'Rubbish. I detest him,' she muttered under her breath as she crossed the yard and headed for the greenhouses.

When Carter joined her there five minutes later, he was carrying three mugs of tea. For a moment she was tempted to refuse the one he offered her, but with John looking on she was reluctant to make her animosity towards Carter too obvious.

It had been almost three months since she had last visited her parents. On that occasion, her visit had been a hurried one in the company of Peter, who had been anxious to remind her that they had promised to visit his own parents the following week. In fact he had reminded her of this so often that she had actually begun to feel rather uncomfortable, as though in some way Peter was trying to suggest that their forthcoming visit to his parents was somehow of greater importance than this brief one to her own.

Because of this, on that occasion she hadn't been able to concentrate as much as she would have liked on her parents' talk of their plans for extending their operation, but now, as she followed the two men into the greenhouses, she was astonished to see how much had been done.

The area under glass, which she remembered as rather small, now seemed to stretch for three times its original distance, and the scent of growing, ripening tomatoes in this first section under glass was dizzyingly mouthwatering. Her grandfather used to grow tomatoes, she remembered, the scent suddenly transporting her back to her early childhood and the quiet, elderly man who had had such patience with her small fingers and impatient questions. He had died before her fifth birthday, but she was surprised how strong those memories now were, brought to the surface by the familiar and evocative scent of the greenhouse.

'Your parents are hoping to instal an automatic watering system in here soon. Luckily, between us we've managed to rig up something that works almost as well for the moment. Just as long as there's someone here to turn on the tap. Which is just here.'

Reminding herself that she was here to learn and work, not to indulge in childhood memories, Elspeth concentrated on what Carter was showing her. As a farmer's daughter she didn't need underlining what could happen if these growing things were deprived of water. She shuddered a little inside, imagining the havoc which would be wreaked if someone was careless enough to forget to water these precious plants, especially in the present mini heat wave.

'Some of the big growers actually use computers to control their watering and ventilation. That's a bit beyond your parents' resources at the moment, but some day....'

'What happens about ventilation at the moment?' Elspeth asked him sharply. They weren't out of June yet, and despite the heat it was still feasible this far north that they could have an overnight frost.

'We've installed a system which rings a warning bell inside the house if the temperature starts to drop beneath a certain point.'

'Which means?' Elspeth pressed.

'Which means that someone has to get out of bed and come down here, close the windows, and if necessary light the heaters, although hopefully we should be past that stage now.'

By the time they had worked their way through the greenhouse, Elspeth watching sharp-eyed while Carter worked. She had to admit fairly that he was scrupulous about everything he did, checking and re-checking. But that was while *she* was here. How did she know what he was doing when she wasn't? Even if he didn't destroy her parents' crop by judiciously forgetting to water or ventilate, what was to stop him giving the growing plants a lethal dose of some chemical or other, which would totally discredit her parents as providers of pure, organically grown produce? Once their reputation was gone, it would be impossible for them to retrieve it; who would ever believe that a competitor, especially one as plausible and seemingly as helpful as Carter, could do such a thing?

By the time they had worked their way outside to where the open beds of vegetables and herbs were growing, the sun had gone from that part of the land, leaving it in shadow.

Quickly Carter showed her how to operate the sprinklers and sprayers which carried the much-needed moisture to the growing plants, at the same time thoroughly checking for any kind of infestation which might destroy the crops.

'Mum told me that she was collecting as many traditional remedies for dealing with bugs and diseases as she could,' Elspeth commented, her enthusiasm caught, her hostility fading despite her attempts to hold on to it. And besides, concentrating on the crops helped to divert her mind away from the mesmeric sight of Carter's sinewy arms in his short-sleeved shirt, of Carter's hard thigh, as he bent down to inspect row after straight row of young green beans, picking one and holding it under the sprinkler before handing it to her and saying with a grin,

'Go on, eat it—it won't poison you.'

'It seems so cruel,' Elspeth objected, and then flushed in acknowledgement of the childishness of her comment as he laughed. Not at her, she noticed, unable to tear her gaze away from the small lines fanning out from his eyes, the warm and generous curve of his mouth. His mouth... Where did it come from, this yearning to reach out and touch it, to trace its contours with the tip of her finger and then with the tip of her tongue? A sensation like a jolt of lightning twisted through her body.

Carter was still holding the vegetable. 'Come on,' he coaxed. 'Just take a bite.'

She reached out for the bean, but somehow or other her fingers closed instead around his wrist, and she discovered that instead of it being her hand that carried the tender vegetable to her lips, it was his, and that, despite the tight grip of her fingers, there was nothing she could do to stop him. She opened her mouth automatically, biting into the firm flesh of the bean, and then tensing in surprise as she discovered how wonderful it tasted.

'It makes all the difference in the world when it's the real thing, doesn't it?' she heard Carter saying, and for a moment she didn't realise he was referring to the bean, but thought—— Quickly she swallowed, trying to pull herself together, trying to remind herself why she was here and what Carter was.

It surprised her how long it took to finish all the watering, and that was only a small part of her parents' day's work. The neatly organised beds had to be kept free of weeds, the growing vegetables constantly checked, watched over.

'Your mother talks to them,' Carter told her as they walked back to the house. 'She claims that they like to feel loved.'

Yes, she could imagine her mother saying that. Her mother firmly believed that everything and everyone needed love.

'So who's telling them that they're loved in her absence?' Elspeth asked flippantly, trying and failing to imagine Carter performing such a task.

'No one as yet,' he informed her so promptly that she stopped to give him a suspicious and hard look.

'You're not suggesting that *I* should start talking to them, are you?' she challenged him.

'Well, you have eaten one of them . . . and in full view of the others,' he reminded her seriously.

'They're probably too terrified of you to listen to you now. Your mother makes a point of never telling them where they're going. She says she doesn't want to frighten the little ones.'

'You're making this up,' Elspeth accused, trying not to laugh.

'That's better,' he told her softly, thoroughly confounding her as he added gravely, 'Your mouth was made for smiles, Elspeth. Smiles and kisses.'

What was he trying to do? Flirt with her? If so, then it was high time she reminded him that she was committed to someone else—or was he simply trying to make fun of her, to confound and deceive her? Did he really think she was stupid enough to fall into that kind of trap, no matter how temptingly it was baited?

How *temptingly*? What on earth was she thinking? That it would be heaven on earth to run her fingertip down that bared male forearm and trace the shape of its muscles... For a moment her imagination swung crazily out of control so that she was mentally reliving this morning's kiss. Reliving it, and actually yearning for it to be repeated.

This *was* madness, she told herself. Complete and utter madness. She had no idea how it had happened either. One moment she had been sternly and firmly reminding herself that Carter was a devious and dangerous man, the next... the next she had focused briefly on his body and had suddenly been swept away into such dangerous and turbulent waters that she was fighting to find a safe foothold.

Thank goodness she had always been the practical, sensible type, not the type to give in to her own emotions, her own foolishness—that side of her nature was something she had brought firmly under control a long time ago.

As they walked into the yard, the dogs came bounding up to them, giving her a welcome excuse not to make any retort to his extraordinary comment as she bent down to fuss them and asked him as naturally as she could, 'What about feeding these two?'

'Yes, I suppose we'd better, and the goats as well. Do you know the routine or should I do it?'

'I think I can manage,' Elspeth told him, anxious to be free of the dangerous potency of his presence.

'Well, if you're sure... I'll go in and shower, and then start on supper. Chicken salad OK for you?'

'Fine,' Elspeth agreed, too surprised by his offer to make supper to offer any objections. That was something Peter would never have offered to do. In fact Peter's mother had already made it plain to Elspeth that, despite the fact that she would continue to work after their marriage, it would be her duty to take care of Peter as devotedly as she, his mother, had always done. That had irked her a little, especially when Peter had smugly reinforced his mother's opinion. But she had decided that it was an issue she would take up with him later, once they were married, gently making it plain to him that they were partners in all things and that included their domestic duties. Now to hear such a male man as Carter calmly suggesting that he make their supper made her blink and stare a little at him.

'What's wrong?' he asked her quizzically. 'Had second thoughts about the chicken?'

'What? Oh, no—I was just wondering about the goats,' she fibbed quickly. 'Who's going to milk them?'

'Oh, that's John's task,' Carter assured her. 'There are a good many things I'm prepared to do for your mother, but milking that precious pair is not among them.'

He said this with such feeling that Elspeth laughed. She knew how troublesome and truculent her mother's spoiled pets could be.

As she heard the sound of her own laughter, she realised how long it had been since she had laughed so freely, since she had felt so... so unconstricted, so free to be herself and not to fall into line with someone else's image of her. And yet who was it who had forced those images on her? she asked herself frowningly as she left Carter to have his shower and started to prepare the dogs' food.

It had been herself, surely. *She* had been the one who had insisted that she wanted a city life, a high-profile career. *She* had been the one to force herself into that mould, and no one else. But why?

Surely not because a thoughtless, silly, empty-headed girl had made fun of her parents' way of life. Surely *that* wasn't what had made her decide to prove to the rest of the world that, despite her upbringing, she could be just as clever, just as career-orientated, just as successful as someone from a different background.

Startled by the direction of her own thoughts, she stopped what she was doing and stared emptily into space.

But she was happy with her chosen life, wasn't she? Content with all that she had achieved, all she would achieve, her job, her flat, her relationship with Peter, the life they had planned together?

Would she *really* prefer to be living here with her parents, sharing their haphazard lives, sharing their hopes and their disappointments, their tears and their laughter?

Something quickened inside her, a feeling that was a combination of joy, pain and regret, and with it came an unwanted recognition that somehow, somewhere, she had perhaps allowed her life to take a wrong turning, that the reason she always felt this odd reluctance to come home, this defensiveness with which she sometimes deliberately shut out her parents, sprang from a very real fear that if she stayed too long, said too much, she might never be able to force herself to go back to the life she had chosen for herself.

As clearly as though they were being spoken now beside her, she heard the high-pitched, cruel words of that girl she had brought home with her.

'Her parents are complete country bumpkins. You wouldn't believe it, honestly... And the house—my dears, I don't think her mother even possesses a vacuum cleaner, never mind knows how to use it. There were actually animals wandering around in the kitchen—imagine! The lack of hygiene... And *she's* just the same, for all that she pretends not to be. One morning I actually found her feeding a lamb with a bottle. She was nursing it on her knee while she ate her own breakfast at the same time. The germs! My dears, my skin was positively crawling when I left. You just can't believe...'

And on and on it had gone, until she hadn't been able to endure any more. And yet now, replaying those words, listening to them with the ears of maturity, she heard more than their surface cruelty, saw more of what might have lain behind them. Sophy had come from a broken home. Her parents were divorced, her father remarried with a much younger second family, her mother living somewhere in America. Neither of them, it seemed, wanted to know about their shared daughter. Sophy's background couldn't have been more different from her own, and she, like the credulous fool she was, had been impressed by the other girl's stories of her parents' seemingly exciting lives, not realising until it was too late how little of that excitement Sophy herself actually shared... How much her own parents' love and care was to be valued and cherished.

Was it really for that, for the desire, the need, the thirst to prove something to someone who had been little more than a lonely child crying out for love and attention herself, that she had redirected the whole course of her life?

But *she* was happy, wasn't she? Wasn't she? She couldn't possibly want to change things—could she? No—no, of course not. Of course she couldn't, she told herself quickly. What she was doing was just indulging in a fit of nostalgia for the country. It was a very fashionable pastime these days. Once she got back to London she would laugh at herself for what she was feeling now. Of course she would. Of course she would... Wouldn't she?

CHAPTER SEVEN

'SUPPER won't be long.'

As she opened the back door, Elspeth saw that Carter was standing in front of the sink washing a lettuce. He had obviously had a shower because, rather disconcertingly, he was barefoot and barechested, wearing only a pair of clean, worn jeans, his hair still damp and slicked back off his face, but the smile he gave her as she came in was casual and easy, completely free of any kind of sexual undertones.

She wasn't sure she wanted to analyse why instead of reassuring her this should make her feel slightly piqued.

'I forgot to mention it earlier,' he added, 'but tomorrow is one of our days for getting orders ready for collection, which means a very early start, I'm afraid. Watering at five, picking at six. There's no need for you to get up if you don't feel up to it, but I'm just warning you in case I disturb you and you wonder what on earth's going on.'

The moment he suggested that she need not get up, Elspeth felt her ire rising. She wasn't a visitor here, to be cosseted and indulged. She was family. *He* was the one who was the outsider, not she.

As the thought formed, she frowned suddenly, remembering an incident from their first meeting, from that summer when her aunt had first introduced him to the family. She had rejected all his overtures of friendship, she remembered; she had felt as though he was patronising her and she had resented it—resented him—resented the fact that her parents had treated him as an adult while they were still treating her as a child, and that had been like gall to her fourteen-year-old emergent pride. Then too she had considered him an outsider—only then she had vocalised her resentment, and had received a lecture from her parents for her pains.

'Pretty basic, I'm afraid,' she heard Carter saying cheerfully as he brought a bowl of crisp lettuce over to the table, 'but I doubt you'd find anything that tastes as good in any of your fancy London restaurants.'

Elspeth suspected he was probably right, but instead of agreeing with him she said contrarily, 'You'd be surprised. All good restaurants these days are conscious of their clientele's desire for healthier eating.'

Carter shrugged as though the subject no longer interested him, indicating the table with its clean cloth and her mother's blue and white china. 'Come and sit down,' he instructed her.

Elspeth saw that in addition to the lettuce and other home-grown salad ingredients, including some deliciously mouthwatering-smelling tomatoes, there was some of her mother's home-cured ham, the bread which she baked every week and a large bowl of fresh fruit.

'Your parents don't have the space for much fruit,' Carter told her, seeing her eyeing the fruit, 'but if I succeed at auction I'm hoping to experiment with fruit under glass.'

'Won't that be very expensive?' Elspeth challenged.

'Mmm. But when I left the institute they gave me a generous pay-off. Banks are much more lenient these days about lending money to small businesses. With the vegetable side to carry me, I can afford to take a small risk.'

Especially if he already had the benefit of her parents' business, Elspeth thought bitterly, as he pulled out a chair for her. For a moment she was tempted to ignore it and walk round to the other side of the table, but to do so would be churlish and non-productive. If she really wanted to find out what he was planning, it would be far easier if he didn't realise how suspicious of him she was.

He was so different from Peter, she reflected as she sat down. Peter would never have prepared a meal like this, nor taken it as a matter of course that he should do so, and Peter would certainly never have sat down to eat wearing only a pair of worn jeans.

She was sitting so close to him that it was impossible for her not to be aware of the fresh, clean scent of his skin. She recognised the distinctive smell of the Pears soap her mother always used, but mingled with it was the elusive and very disturbing fragrance that was his alone. It took on an erotic and dangerous allure that made her wish that she was sitting further away from him.

Unlike her, Carter seemed totally undisturbed by any such awareness. He might just as well have been fully dressed rather than virtually naked, she reflected angrily, wishing she had the courage to put a little more distance between them. It was totally ridiculous, but the harder she tried to ignore her awareness of him, the more intense it became, until her shoulders and back were tight with tension, and she was fighting not to look at him...

What was it about this particular man that made it such a wanton pleasure merely to absorb visually the physical reality of him? But she didn't merely want to *look* at him, she recognised on a tiny shiver. She wanted to reach out and touch him. She wanted...

What on earth was happening to her? she wondered miserably, doggedly trying to concentrate on the food on her plate.

She was so deeply engrossed in her own bewildering emotions that it was doubly unnerving to hear Jasper suddenly say mournfully, in a very creditable impersonation of her father's slow tones, 'Pity about Elspeth... She needs a good man.'

Horrified, Elspeth stared transfixed at the wretched bird, clenching her hands so that she couldn't give in to the unbearable temptation to get up and wring its neck. At the same time, she was conscious of the slow burn of colour heating her skin as anger and embarrassment filled her with equal intensity.

It was one thing to know in her most secret heart that her parents, while accepting her choice of Peter, could quite genuinely not understand what attracted her to him—it was quite another to have that appalling parrot voice their doubts in front of Carter.

For what seemed like an endless stretch of time she waited with pent-up breath and feelings for him to make some mocking comment, and then, when she realised that he wasn't going to do so, that he was diplomatically going to pretend that Jasper had never uttered those betraying words, instead of being relieved, grateful to him for his tact, all she felt was a growing, choking rage, which exploded forcefully inside her, making her stand up abruptly, pushing her chair back with a rough, scraping sound, her voice shaking with temper and pain as she said bitterly, 'Why don't you go ahead and laugh? I'm sure you want to—but *I* happen to love Peter and he loves me.'

She stopped abruptly, knowing that if she said any more she was liable to burst into tears. What was the matter with her, why did she feel this need to justify herself, her relationship with Peter, and to this man who meant nothing to her, had no place in her life? Had he been there while her parents were discussing Peter? Had he been privy to their doubts and concern? It hurt her more than she could bear to think that he had. It was almost as though it was a kind of betrayal.

'Look, Elspeth . . .'

Was that pity she could hear in his voice? Her body stiffened as she rejected the hand he was placing on her arm. 'Don't touch me,' she demanded chokily. 'And in future perhaps you'd be good enough to refrain from wandering around half naked.'

She saw his face change, his eyebrows lifting, something almost approaching amusement lightening his eyes. 'Oh, come on. You aren't trying to tell me that you aren't used to the sight of a bare male chest. After all, you and Peter are virtually engaged.'

'That's different,' Elspeth told him fiercely, 'and besides, contrary to what you seem to imagine, Peter and I are not——' She stopped abruptly, her face suddenly bright with colour.

'Go on,' Carter encouraged, marvellously self-assured where she suddenly felt as gauche and miserable as a child. 'You and Peter aren't what?'

'Nothing,' Elspeth said stubbornly.

'You aren't lovers, is that what you were going to say?' he pressed, ignoring her.

Suddenly it was all too much for her. She had never experienced so many contradictory and see-sawing emotions in such a short space of time. Never had her ideals, her beliefs, her feelings been challenged so thoroughly nor so frighteningly, never had she felt them slip away so far out of her own control.

'There's no need to sound so amused,' she told him bitterly. 'Not all men are obsessed with sex. There are other equally important aspects to relationships.'

'I agree that sex on its own is never a good basis on which to form a good relationship, but there is a difference between being obsessed with sex and not having any interest in it at all. If I were a woman I think I should be a little concerned at the thought of committing myself to life with a man who seemed not to find me sexually desirable.'

Elspeth felt the breath leak out of her lungs on a painful sob. How dared he say that? How dared he suggest that Peter didn't want her? And yet— and yet—wasn't it what she had sometimes said to herself alone and awake at night, wondering a little uncomfortably why it was that Peter should be so content to say goodnight with nothing more than a chaste and hasty kiss, and why she herself should feel something almost approaching relief that he should be? She had thought then that it was be- cause she herself must only have a low sex-drive, that she and Peter were both victims of the modern disease of overwork. And yet when Carter had kissed her in that brief, illuminating space of time, she had recognised and felt all those things, all those emotions, all those needs and desires, which she had been telling herself it was impossible for her to feel. Too late now to wish she had never gained that knowledge, that she had remained safe in her illusion that she was incapable of feeling such desire.

Now she went white with pain as she lied des- perately, 'Peter *does* want me. He's... He's just too much of a gentleman to—to force me into— into something I'm not ready for.'

Carter gave her a brief, hard look. 'So you're the one who doesn't want him. And you still intend to marry him. Why?'

Elspeth was literally trembling now, not just with anger, but with anguish as well. How *dared* he challenge her like this, talk to her like this, hurt her like this?

'I don't think that's any of your business,' she told him fiercely, 'and now, if you don't mind...'

She started to turn away, but he caught hold of her, stopping her, swinging her back round to face him.

'Oh, but I do mind,' he told her grittily. 'And I want to know why, when you become all woman in my arms, when you respond so passionately to my kiss, you're going to marry a man who you've just admitted can't turn you on.'

Elspeth went rigid with shock at the brutality of his verbal attack, totally unable to hide her reaction nor to silence the immediate denial that choked from her throat. 'I thought you were Peter,' she lied desperately. 'I didn't want you at all.'

'Is that a fact?'

Suddenly he seemed very intimidating, very male and alien, and suddenly she wished desperately that she were a million miles away from him, and safe from the dark intent she could read in his eyes.

'Let me go, Carter.'

She tried to keep her voice steady, to inject a note of cool lightness into it, to prove to him that she was completely unaffected by what was happening, but her voice shook a little, and she knew quite well he must have felt the tiny tremor that burned through her.

For a moment she actually thought she saw compassion soften his mouth, actually felt that he might out of pity let her go—but suddenly his grasp tightened, his mouth hardening as he looked down at her and said softly, 'Not yet.'

She knew already that he was going to kiss her.

She had a handful of seconds, maybe less, in which to tell herself frantically that this time it would be different, this time she would be prepared, this time there would be no terrifying, unbelievable awareness that under this man's hands, under this man's mouth, every single one of her senses, every smallest nerve-ending flowered and blossomed, and that with them the tightly close-furled bud of sensuality she had never known she possessed burst into life inside her.

A handful of seconds. Such a small space of time, so why instead of using it did she simply stand within his arms, trembling not with apprehension, nor even with anger, but with a sensation which she dimly recognised as being born of the quick, wanton heat that filled her whole body? The traitor within, she recognised dizzily as her lips parted in instinctive response to the hard heat of his.

And yet it wasn't a violent kiss, nor yet even an angry kiss—not a punishment at all really, despite the volcanic threat of his words.

She protested once as she fought against his sensual domination of her body, and instantly his mouth lifted, but when she attempted to turn her head aside he checked the movement, not aggressively, but with the gentle strength of his open palm cupping her jaw, stroking the softness of her skin, so that she looked at him with unknowingly tormented and bewildered eyes, shivering beneath the explosion of emotions he was generating, her senses obedient to the silent demand of his, so that this time when he kissed her she automatically moved closer to him, instinctively and unknowingly slid her arms around his neck, and sighed tremulously beneath the pressure of his mouth, inviting the male possession of it in a dozen subtle and unintended ways.

People didn't kiss like this; not grown-up, adult people, she thought hazily at some point. This kind of kissing was for impossibly romantic films and besotted teenagers.

Adults were intimate, made love, had sex, their kisses a brief tactical opening-stage towards that goal; but this kiss . . . this kiss was a whole world of sensation and delight complete unto itself.

She couldn't remember that she hadn't wanted him to touch her, only that now she couldn't bear him to stop; that each time he left her mouth to nibble the soft flesh of her ear, each time he bit gently at her bottom lip and teased her with the soft stroke of his tongue, she grew more hungry, more desirous, more shockingly eager for the return of his mouth to hers, clinging urgently to its possession.

When he finally set her free it was the sound of her own incoherent denial of that freedom that shocked her back to awareness, her eyes opening into his in bewildered pain, her body trembling and so weak that she felt as though she had no physical strength at all.

From a distance she heard Carter saying in a strained voice, 'I'm sorry. I never intended . . .'

And brutally she came back to reality and realised what she had done.

She felt quite sick with mortification. No wonder Carter sounded so embarrassed. No wonder he was keeping his back to her.

Valiantly she struggled for something to say, for some light, insouciant words that would somehow or other return everything to normal. She tried to imagine herself saying airily something or other about missing Peter and apologising for getting a little carried away, and knew helplessly that she could never make that kind of lie sound anything like believable.

Now, when oddly enough she hadn't been particularly aware of it at the time, her body was shockingly telling her how much it missed its intimate contact with Carter's. How much it longed for the sensation of that hard male flesh in intimate contact with her own. Frantically she closed her eyes, trying to banish the shocking images dancing in her head, but they refused to go away.

She heard Carter saying her name in an uncomfortable, strained voice. Instinctively she turned to look at him, and then wished she hadn't. Heaven alone knew what he must have read in her expression to make his own change like that, to make him look at her so blankly and so grimly, as though he wanted to shut out the image of her forever.

It wasn't all *her* fault—*she* hadn't been the one who had initiated the kiss, even if she... She gulped painfully and bit her bottom lip to stop its wild trembling.

'For God's sake.'

The raw, furious male sound was like knives tearing at her flesh. Unable to endure any more, she did something she had never in her life imagined herself doing; she swung round and ran betrayingly and desperately towards the inner door, opening it before Carter could stop her and fleeing for the sanctuary of her borrowed bedroom.

In the kitchen Carter stared after her, and then into the silence the parrot, who had taken in the whole scene with avid curiosity, repeated with un-nerving accuracy and emotion something which neither Elspeth herself nor Carter had even realised she had said, something so emotional and be-traying that Carter blenched as the bird whispered emotively and pleadingly, 'Carter.'

There was nothing else but that one word—his name, repeated so exactly as Elspeth had unknow-ingly whispered it when she had pleaded for the return of his mouth to hers that the hairs on his arms stood sharply erect and his body responded so savagely and so achingly that he took a step to-wards the parrot and told him bitterly, 'Don't you ever, ever do that again, otherwise...'

'Nice chap, Carter,' the parrot told him palli-atively. 'Like him very much. Pity about Elspeth,' he added mournfully, strategically getting out of Carter's reach. 'Pity about Elspeth.'

Upstairs Elspeth sat with her head in her hands, trying to come to terms with what she had done, with what she had allowed to happen.

Useless to try to pretend any more. Physically Carter aroused her as a woman as she had never dreamed any man could arouse her. If there in the kitchen he had whispered to her that he wanted to make love to her ... If he had caressed her, touched her, if he had slid the clothes from her body and then touched her naked flesh with his hands and then his mouth ...

She trembled violently at the very thought. Appalled by what she was thinking, and yet at the same time knowing a helpless, sick longing for something far more tangible than the mere mental knowledge of how she would feel if Carter *had* made love to her.

Now, when she was completely alone, when he wasn't touching her in any way at all, when she ought to have been safely free of whatever spell it was he cast over her, she was yearning, aching, wanting him in such an earthy and elemental way that she could hardly comprehend that she was actually having these feelings.

She wanted Carter to make love to her. She said the words silently to herself, half expecting them to be followed by a rush of mental denial—but nothing happened, apart from the fact that that dull, unfamiliar ache way down in the pit of her stomach seemed to twist fiercely and burn.

She shivered, suddenly feeling cold, shocked that she could feel like this, and for a man who didn't desire her, didn't love her. For a man who had done nothing to encourage her to feel like this.

No, right from the start she had been the one who had for some reason made his presence in her life take on a sensual significance. Right from the very start, when she had been so sure he had been trying to flirt with her, when she had failed to recognise him, and in so doing had—what?— sprung the trap into which she had now fallen.

It would be different once Peter got here, she told herself firmly. Once Peter was here, all this non-sense would stop. She would be her normal self again. Perhaps she might even suggest to Peter that it was time they set a formal date for the wedding. Yes, perhaps that was it. Because she could not allow herself to think of Peter in such sensual terms, her mind was playing tricks on her and transferring her burgeoning desire to Carter.

She frowned. *Why* couldn't she think of Peter as her lover? They *were* after all going to be married. There was no reason why they should not be lovers. It was all very well being sensible, she decided for-lornly, but this evening, in Carter's arms, beneath Carter's mouth, her senses had been awakened to such aching pleasures that the thought of being sensible, cautious and pragmatic suddenly had no appeal at all.

She closed her eyes, and tried to visualise Peter behaving as Carter had. Sweeping her into his arms, kissing her with the same strong male passion, turning her body into molten heat, making her want him so much that she began to make soft, sweetly pleading noises beneath his mouth.

Perhaps there was something wrong with her imagination, she decided dispiritedly five minutes later, opening her eyes and bitterly admitting that she just could not visualise Peter and herself in such a situation.

But she did love him. Of course she did. And he loved her, and they were going to be married.

And tomorrow morning she would pretend she had overslept and that way with a bit of luck she wouldn't have to face Carter again until after he came back from his auction. By that time she was sure she would be in a much more sensible frame of mind. Back to her normal self.

It was only later when she crawled into bed, feeling more confused and unhappy than she could ever remember feeling in her life, that she wondered miserably if she would ever be her old 'normal' self again.

A vast chasm seemed to have appeared between the Elspeth with whom she was so familiar and whom she thought she knew so well, and this new one, whom she did not know at all, and whom, she was beginning to discover, that part of the old Elspeth which remained found extremely frightening.

The trouble with this new Elspeth was that she had a whole set of emotions, a whole range of awareness and senses that the old Elspeth had never experienced in her life.

The best thing she could do was to somehow or other banish this new Elspeth before she began to get too much of a hold on her, Elspeth decided tiredly. Yes, that was what she must do. Starting with tomorrow, she must firmly force herself back into her familiar, businesslike mould. This new Elspeth must not be allowed to get a hold on her. She was far too disruptive, far too illogical, far too vulnerable. Far, far too vulnerable.

CHAPTER EIGHT

IT WAS the warning burr of her parents' radio alarm that woke Elspeth from her confused and painful dreams to lie disorientated and unrefreshed while she tried to grapple with why on earth she had ever set the alarm for four-thirty. Reluctantly she had to admit that, if she had to wake up at such an unholy hour, she couldn't have chosen a better morning on which to do so.

The rising sun shone in through the window from a clear pale blue sky, as she discovered once she had forced herself out of bed. It was, she recognised sleepily, going to be a perfect summer's day.

Long ago memories of distant summers, of waking early so that she could help with some of the farm chores before setting out for school, came back to her so sharply and nostalgically that for a moment, standing in front of the window, breathing in the country-scented air, she forgot how early it was, and remembered only that she had willingly swapped all this to live in a city.

For years she had told herself stoically that she didn't miss the country, that she preferred the hectic pace of city life, that those who talked nostalgically and enviously of living in the country were thinking only of a picture-postcard countryside which bore no resemblance whatsoever to reality. In winter, country lanes were ankle-deep in mud, country gardens bleak, dank, empty spaces, country houses damp and cold; and yet there were other mornings, crisp with frost when the air was sharply scented with the promise of snow, autumn days when the gales buffeted the trees and dared human beings to challenge their strength, and days like these when a heat haze already misted the distant hills and the air was already warm and scented.

She wasn't here to daydream about the weather, though—she was here to work. Last night she had told herself it would be the easiest thing in the world to simply stay in bed this morning and so avoid having to face Carter, but she had resolutely denied herself that escape route.

She was going to show him that no matter how bitterly she might regret what had happened, no matter how self-contemptuous she might feel, she was not afraid to face him. Like a dose of nasty medicine, the sooner it was over with the better, and hopefully they would be so busy working that she wouldn't have to do anything more than distantly acknowledge his presence.

She showered and then dressed quickly in a pair of ancient denim shorts and a comfortable, loose T-shirt—clothes which she would never have dreamed of wearing in London, nor in the immaculate suburban garden that belonged to Peter's parents. In fact these clothes belonged to the years before she had left home for London.

Quickly brushing her hair, and applying some protective moisturiser to her face, she pulled on a pair of shabby trainers and opened her bedroom door.

Was Carter still in bed? Resolutely she walked past the closed bedroom door and went downstairs. As she opened the kitchen door she smelled the freshly made coffee and hesitated in the open doorway, but Carter had already heard her. He turned round, not quite masking his surprise, and then frowning as he looked rather piercingly at her.

She withstood his look as steadily as she could, but her voice wasn't quite as easy to control as she said shakily, 'You did say you wanted an early start this morning!'

'Yes, but I didn't mean that you had to join us.'

'That's what I'm here for,' she told him grimly. If privately she was beginning to realise that three days would never have been sufficient for her parents to educate her in all that needed doing just to keep the business ticking over, she was not going to admit as much to anyone else. And especially not to him.

The parrot, for some obscure reason, was whistling the 'Marseillaise', but as she approached the table he stopped to comment admiringly, 'Nice legs.'

When Elspeth glowered at him, Carter told her smoothly, 'He's had a rather chequered career. I believe he was about to become the victim of a broken home when your mother rescued him.'

'I'm not surprised,' Elspeth retorted scathingly, still glowering at the bird, who was now preening himself. 'I wouldn't even be surprised if he was the cause of the broken home.'

'Coffee?' Carter invited, indicating the filter jug. 'I've had my breakfast, but if you'd like some toast——'

'If I want toast I'm perfectly capable of making my own,' Elspeth told him acidly.

Why didn't he just go away and leave her alone? He must realise how uncomfortable she felt with him now, how—how mortified and embarrassed. Just because he was behaving as though nothing out of the ordinary had happened it didn't mean that she found it as easy to put last night out of her mind. She looked at him suspiciously, wondering if he was deliberately baiting her by behaving so perfectly normally, or was there a more sinister reason behind his apparent pleasantness? Was he concerned that because of last night she might insist on his leaving the house, and in doing so make it more difficult for him to sabotage her parents' work? She had every right to ask him to go, she reflected bitterly, as she poured herself some coffee, taking care to give him as wide a berth as possible as she walked past him.

His behaviour towards her had been atrocious. There was nothing she would like more than for him to leave, but she dared not confront him; she was too frightened that he might retaliate by claiming that she wanted him to go not because he had kissed her against her will, but because she had wanted him to kiss her.

She knew if he made that accusation that there was no way she could deny it. If he had been a gentleman he would have left without her having to say anything, she thought, tight-lipped, but then if he'd been a gentleman he would never have done it in the first place.

Peter would never in a thousand years have behaved in such a way.

She sipped her coffee and then tensed, as she realised in outrage that it was not gratitude for Peter's reserve that was colouring her thoughts, but a certain rebellious wistfulness that made her frown angrily and curse her own stupidity.

She was just finishing her coffee when a battered van pulled into the yard, sending the dogs into a frenzy of barking and scattering the scratching hens.

'That will be John and Simon,' Carter announced. 'I'll leave you to finish your breakfast in peace. No need to hurry.'

No need to hurry because he didn't want her to see what he might be doing, Elspeth reflected darkly as he opened the back door. She was suddenly discovering that she had an unexpectedly vivid imagination, which relayed to her pictures of her mother's tender baby carrots and peas, with all their careful organic nurturing, suddenly being sprinkled with some hideous compound of chemical fertilisers designed to ruin her parents' reputation and their business. And it wouldn't be that difficult— Carter had said something about watering the crops before they picked them.

Ignoring the faint growling noises from her stomach telling her that a piece of toast would be more than welcome, she finished her coffee, grabbed a pair of her mother's gardening gloves from the basket beside the door and hurried after Carter.

The yard was empty of dogs and men and, having automatically thrown out a couple of handfuls of grain for the hens as she walked past, Elspeth followed them.

As she approached the greenhouses and the long rows of vegetables and salads growing out in the open, she saw that the sprinklers were already at work watering the crops. While Carter opened the greenhouse windows, the other two men were steadily removing the tunnels of protective plastic from younger rows of crops.

Carter saw her arrive, and came out of the greenhouse towards her, standing so close to her that she was immediately aware of the warm male scent of him. His skin also carried the rich smell of the greenhouse tomatoes, and she had a dizzying thought that if she were to touch his skin now with her mouth it might taste of the warm, ripe fruit.

Love-apples, wasn't that what the Elizabethans had called tomatoes? She felt her skin suddenly flushing hotly at the direction of her thoughts, unaware of the quick, frowning look Carter gave her as she suddenly stepped hurriedly back from him.

His urgent warning made her freeze, but she had already stepped back on to the rake lying behind her and had started to overbalance.

It was only natural that he should reach out and grab hold of her to steady her, an instinctive and automatically protective gesture that anyone might have made, but the minute his fingers closed round the smooth flesh of her arms she was aware of him so intensely and intimately that she could hardly breathe for the choking ache of need that flared through her whole body.

Her violent, 'Don't touch me,' was borne out of her own shocked fear that he would see just how much she ached for exactly the opposite, but he reacted to it immediately, letting go of her arm as though her flesh burned him—or disgusted him, she thought tormentedly.

She felt sick and dizzy, oddly light-headed as though she had been standing out in the sun for too long, filled with unwanted yearnings and needs.

'Where do you want us to start, Carter?'

Neither of them had heard John approaching, and Elspeth turned away instinctively as Carter looked away from her; she hid her face in the shadows, terrified of what anyone might read in it.

'Er—I think we'd better start with the carrots, and then there's the peas.'

'I'll do those,' Elspeth offered quickly. Anything, anything to get away from Carter, to be somewhere where she didn't have to look at him.

He gave her a brief nod in acceptance of her offer, apparently as reluctant to look at her as she was to look at him.

As she walked away from him, she was conscious of a certain stiffness in her movements, a deep and desperate tension within her body.

Picking peas might not be the most mentally challenging task in the world, but it was certainly therapeutic, she acknowledged ten minutes later, surprised and pleased by how quickly she had discovered the forgotten rhythms of her childhood, the forgotten instructions of her mother, so that she was automatically discarding those pods that were as yet too small, swiftly developing a skill which had her basket soon filled and another started.

As she worked doggedly among the peas, refusing to turn round and look for Carter, she tried to tell herself that what she was experiencing was just some kind of aberration—a form of pre-marital nerves.

Only she wasn't the nervy type, and she and Peter had still not yet finally set a date for the wedding. So what was wrong with her? Why was she experiencing these unfamiliar longings, these disruptive needs which had never previously featured in her life?

'Everything OK here?'

She tensed, her hand trembling as she heard Carter's voice behind her. Resolutely refusing to turn round or to acknowledge the soft, almost caring note in his voice, she kept her back to him and said curtly, 'Yes.'

She could still feel his presence behind her, as though he was waiting for something. The skin at the back of her neck prickled dangerously. Suddenly sweat broke out on her skin. The heat of the sun, she told herself chokily, even though before Carter's arrival its early morning warmth had not bothered her at all.

'Elspeth.'

Her muscles locked. If he touched her now, if he placed his hands on her shoulders and turned her round to face him, if he looked into her eyes, searched her face... if he bent his head until she could feel the warmth of his breath against her skin. He would taste of toothpaste and coffee; his mouth would be warm and male and the taste of it would make her go faint and dizzy with pleasure.

'Elspeth, are you all right?'

She realised sickly that she was actually swaying towards him, that her body, already visibly aroused by her own thoughts, was yearning towards him as though to the pull of a magnet.

'You shouldn't have got up so early. There was no need,' she heard Carter saying roughly. 'You aren't used to this kind of life. I should never...'

It was too much. Something inside her suddenly snapped and she turned on him and said shakily, 'You should never have kissed me—is that what you were going to say? Well, you're quite right, you should not, and I wish more than anything else in the world that you *had* not, but if you think that just because you *did* kiss me that I'm incapable of doing anything other than swooning at your feet in gratitude then think again. And now, if you wouldn't mind leaving me alone, perhaps I could get on with what I'm doing.'

She saw that he was staring at her as though he'd never really seen her before, and no wonder, she thought numbly. She was behaving like a virago, like a fool, like a woman in love. A woman in love.

She felt the rush of sensation burn through her, heard the distant sound of a car arriving, heard the bark of the dogs and the confusion of car doors opening, but it all seemed to be happening on another level, in another place. She was incapable of doing anything other than standing transfixed while she tried to grapple with her own confused thoughts. A woman in love. Well, that was what she was, wasn't she? She was in love with Peter.

Only she and Peter had always said seriously and firmly that they were not 'in love'; that being 'in love' was not a state they desired. They were good friends, they cared deeply for one another, and when they married their marriage would be successful because it was not confused by emotions that might ultimately fade. People in love were people who were suffering a kind of madness.

A kind of madness . . . was that it—was she going mad? She looked at Carter with bewildered, anguished eyes, but he was already looking away from her and saying quickly, 'I must go. Someone's just arrived.'

Someone had, as Elspeth saw—a slender blonde woman was hurrying towards them, her face breaking into a warm smile as she spotted Carter.

'Carter, how wonderful to see you!' she called out eagerly. 'You're very naughty, you know. You promised to come over for dinner and you still haven't done. I'm dying to show off my new house to you. I'm glad now that I offered to come over this morning and collect our stuff. Is it ready now or am I too early?'

Elspeth turned back to her peas, not wanting to watch Carter returning the blonde's comments. Not wanting to see what? Carter taking another woman in his arms, kissing her as he had kissed . . . But no—she wasn't going to allow her thoughts to stray down that road, not again. It was too painful, too self-revealing, too dangerous.

In the distance she could still hear the woman talking to Carter, her light, flirtatious tones mingling with his deeper, very male voice. She laughed, the sound setting Elspeth's teeth on edge.

They were coming towards her, she recognised, desperately trying to lose herself at the back of the pea sticks.

'So you won't forget. We're expecting you for dinner just as soon as Kate and Richard get back.'

'I'm looking forward to it,' Carter assured her.

We... Elspeth's heart thumped. Did that mean the woman was married? If so, what was she doing flirting so outrageously with Carter? she wondered fiercely.

'Oh, and good luck with the auction this afternoon.'

They were moving away again. Thank goodness. Elspeth didn't want to see them together, didn't want to see the other woman's hand resting possessively on Carter's tanned arm, didn't want to see Carter turning towards her, smiling at her.

She bit her lip sharply, trembling with the force of her own emotions. Unwanted emotions, ridiculous emotions, emotions she had no right to feel.

By eleven o'clock Elspeth was exhausted. She had just watched what Carter had said was the last of their customers drive away, and now the men, apparently as full of energy as they had been at five o'clock, were turning to study the depleted rows of produce, while Carter arranged which seedlings were to be transferred from the nursery beds to form fresh new rows.

'Why don't you go in?' he suggested to her, when the two men had moved away. 'It's hot out here, and you aren't ...'

'Aren't what?' she demanded fiercely, her eyes daring him to suggest that her strength was less than his.

'Aren't used to working outside in this kind of heat,' he told her calmly. 'At the very least you ought to be wearing a hat of some sort.' He looked at his watch. 'Look, I've got to be at this auction at two. Why don't we stop now and have an early lunch? You could come with me if you like.'

Go with him. Elspeth stared at him, wondering what on earth had prompted such an invitation. 'I can't,' she told him stiffly. 'I ... I promised I'd ring Peter.'

It wasn't true and there was no way he could know that she was lying, and yet the way he looked at her made her feel that somehow he did.

'Besides,' she added feverishly, 'you said you'd be gone for most of the afternoon and everything will need watering, especially with this heat.'

'Not until later.'

She turned back to her self-imposed task of checking the growth of the new rows of peas, and said as casually as she could, 'You go on ahead. I'm not hungry yet.'

It was a lie—her stomach had been noisily reminding her for the last hour that she hadn't had any breakfast, but the last thing she felt capable of enduring right now was an intimate lunch with Carter.

Out of the corner of her eye she saw his mouth tighten as though he was contemplating arguing with her, and then to her relief he turned on his heel and walked away from her.

He had been gone less than half an hour when she was forced to acknowledge that he had been right and that the combination of no breakfast, hard physical work, and a very hot sun had produced not only a poundingly sick headache, but also a weak, shivery feeling that she very much feared heralded the onset of heat-stroke. But much as she longed to go back to the house and lie down in the coolness of a shaded bedroom, her pride would not allow her to return while Carter was still about.

The auction didn't start until two. That meant he probably didn't need to leave until one. It was eleven-forty-five now, and the sun was getting hotter and stronger by the minute.

She glanced across to where the two men were busily engaged in planting out new rows of carrots and lettuce, their steady, purposeful movements indicative of experience and skill. The low murmur of their voices seemed to buzz disorientatingly in her ears. There was nothing she wanted more than to lie down somewhere cool—yes, there was, she acknowledged thirstily. She wanted a drink...ice-cold, clear water... The more she thought about it, the greater her thirst became. All she needed to do was to stop work and to walk the short distance back to the house. That was all she needed to do.

But if she did that Carter would see her, and for some obscure reason it had become extremely important to her that she stayed here until he had gone.

But how could she? The minutes seemed to crawl by, and she felt more and more peculiar with every one of them, and then unbelievably, as though in answer to a silent prayer, she suddenly heard the kitchen door open, and turned round just in time to see Carter getting into her mother's small red car which he then backed out of the yard.

He had gone. She could go back to the house. For several seconds she stood where she was, watching the lane, holding her breath, half expecting to see him come driving back. But when five and then ten minutes had passed without him doing so, she expelled a shaky breath, and as slowly and carefully as though her body were made of fragile glass she headed back to the house.

Once inside the kitchen she turned on the cold water tap, and leaned heavily against the sink unit while she waited for it to run icy cold. She felt vaguely sick now, shivery as well, and the pain in her head had intensified to the point where she could scarcely see. Her hand shook as she filled a glass with water. She drank it greedily and then drank another. What she needed was to go and lie down for half an hour. But first she had to find something to ease this headache.

She found some tablets in her mother's bathroom and took two of them and then for good measure another two, before stripping off her clothes and going to lie down on the blessedly cool eiderdown.

It was bliss not to move, and even more bliss not to have the full heat of the sun pounding down on her unprotected head. Dizzily she acknowledged that she ought to have made herself some lunch, but the thought of food was now totally nauseating. All she needed was a couple of hours' sleep—that would soon make her feel better. She wasn't used to getting up at five o'clock in the morning any more. In London there was no need for such early country rising. She turned restlessly on the large bed. The bed in her flat was a small single. For some reason her parents' bed seemed to intensify that nagging ache of aloneness, of isolation, which seemed to shadow her constantly these days.

As she drifted off to sleep she reflected that it would be nice to have someone to share a large double bed with, someone solid and masculine, someone with tanned, muscled forearms, and warm, teasing amber eyes...

Someone like Carter. No, not Carter, she corrected herself drowsily, but it was already too late—her imagination had furnished his image so clearly for her that when she turned on her side with a sleepy smile it was Carter she was mentally visualising next to her and not Peter, the man it ought to have been.

She woke up with a start, conscious of cramp in her shoulder muscles, a dull ache in her temples and the inevitable soreness and stiffness of muscles unused to so much outside physical activity.

Moving reluctantly, she glanced at her watch. Five o'clock. Without knowing how she knew, something about the quality of the house's stillness told her that Carter hadn't returned.

She had no idea how much property was being auctioned and had not thought to ask him when he would return, and as she cautiously climbed off the bed, wincing as her sore muscles protested, she told herself that it was a relief to have the house to herself, that she would be more than glad if he chose not to return at all.

She had a bath rather than a shower, hoping the warmth of the water and a generous handful of her mother's bath salts might do something to release the ache from her body.

She still felt physically drained, and very hungry. The dogs would need feeding, she reminded herself as she dressed in a clean T-shirt and her jeans, and so would the rest of the livestock. Since Carter had not seen fit to tell her when he was returning, she suspected she would have to undertake these tasks herself.

It was only when she had finished feeding the goats and checked their tethers that she noticed the newly planted rows of vegetables wilting under the still hot sun. Frowningly she studied them. They needed watering. Carter had told her he would attend to this chore when he got back, but she wasn't a helpless Victorian clinging-vine, incapable of doing anything for herself. She would show him that she was just as capable of doing this task as he. Purposefully she hurried over to the greenhouse, fixing the hosepipe to the outdoor tap and carrying the reel as far as the newly planted beds, where she fastened a sprinkler bar to the pipe and set it firmly in the middle of the area she wanted to water.

Returning to the tap she turned it on and watched with some satisfaction as cooling jets of water, glittering like diamonds in the still-strong sunshine, fell on the thirsty plants. She stayed for a few minutes to check that the sprinkler was working properly and then went back indoors.

There was still no sign of Carter, and she was far too hungry to wait and see if he returned before having something to eat. Besides, why should she wait for him after all? He meant nothing to her, nor she to him. Maybe he had asked her to go with him this afternoon, but he must have had an ulterior motive—he couldn't possibly have wanted her company. Not when he had women like this morning's blonde breathlessly hanging on his every word, she reflected sourly.

She took some eggs from the larder, and broke them into a bowl, discovering as she beat them that she was doing so with a lot more gusto than the task required. Scrambled eggs on toast, a cup of coffee and some fruit. Wonderful.

As she made the scrambled eggs, she acknowledged wryly that Peter would have shown scant enthusiasm for such fare. If Peter had a vice it was that he liked to be seen wining and dining in the right places, and by 'right places' Peter meant the kind of places where he could make the right kind of prestigious business contacts. Sometimes she winced a little to hear him boasting of having dined at the next table to such and such a person, although she had noticed that when he related these incidents to his parents his mother always smiled approvingly, quite plainly delighting in what she was

being told. Was it only her perhaps too-critical ear
that caught the note of almost pompous self-conceit
with which Peter related the over-rich menus, the
variety of wines and the highly inflated prices that
went with them? She herself much preferred simple
food. There were even occasions when she actually
invented excuses to prevent her from accompanying Peter on some of his many business
dinners, she acknowledged guiltily as she spooned
the eggs on to her warm toast and carried the plate
over to the table.

Her head was still aching threateningly, and
although the sky was clear outside she hadn't forgotten that Carter had said thunderstorms were
forecast.

If and when it came she hoped it was at night,
when she could safely bury her head under the bedclothes and cower there unseen. It wasn't so much
the thunder that terrified her but the lightning. Peter
had told her very caustically what he thought of
this childish fear, refusing to even listen when she
had tried to explain that it was an uncontrollable
as it was irrational.

Her parents were far more understanding, and
she knew that her father tended to blame himself
for it because he had had to leave her alone in that
long-ago storm when the lightning had struck and
destroyed the oak tree, while he'd rescued a cow
which had got herself caught on some barbed wire.

Her meal eaten, she washed up and poured
herself a second cup of coffee. She still felt drained
and drowsy, her head tightly banded with tension.
She wanted to rest, but her thoughts wouldn't let

her, driving her to pace the kitchen, stopping constantly to stare out of the window, almost as though she was willing her mother's car to suddenly materialise in the yard with Carter at the wheel.

Which was ridiculous. All she had wanted from the moment she'd arrived and found him here was for him to leave. And now that he had done, albeit only temporarily, she was so restless and edgy that anyone would think she actually missed him.

She had just finished her second cup of coffee and was reluctantly beginning to think that Carter wasn't going to return until later when she heard the sound of a car and saw the bright red bodywork of her mother's convertible coming down the lane.

For some obscure reason, instead of staying where she was in the kitchen she hurried upstairs. She didn't want to give Carter the impression that she was hanging around waiting for him, she told herself firmly. Because, of course, she wasn't doing that. It was just that she had become so used to him being around that she was conscious of his absence.

She heard the car stop and then seconds later the kitchen door open, but when she heard Carter bellowing her name like an enraged bull she stared at the closed bedroom door as though unable to believe her ears.

It wasn't until she heard him pounding upstairs that she actually moved, opening the bedroom door at the same moment as he banged impatiently on it

'Oh, there you are,' he said unnecessarily. He was breathing hard and he looked absolutely furiously angry, she recognised.

'Oh, dear. Didn't you get the farm?' she asked him, immediately suspecting the cause of his fury, but to her surprise he gritted,

'Yes, I got it. What the devil are you playing at, Elspeth? I presume it was *you* who put that sprinkler on, wasn't it?'

Elspeth stared at him, totally confused both by his anger and his question. 'Of course it was me,' she assured him. 'I went out, saw that those poor plants were wilting in the full heat of the sun and naturally I put on the sprinkler. You did say that you would be back in time to do the watering, but——'

'I *am* back in time,' he told her gratingly, and then burst out as though completely unable to stop himself, 'My God, don't you know anything—and you a farmer's daughter? You never—repeat—never water anything when it's in full sunlight.'

Elspeth stared at him, the words of rejection burning on her tongue until suddenly too late, from out of the past, she heard her mother's soft voice explaining gently to her as a child why plants should only be watered when they were in the shade.

It was a novice's mistake, inexcusable in someone of her upbringing, and the thought of the potential damage she could have caused made the colour leave her face. 'I'll go and turn it off,' she muttered, too shocked to attempt to defend herself, but Carter stopped her, putting his arm across the open doorway to bar the exit.

'Oh, no, you don't. That will only compound your stupidity,' he told her acidly. 'The sun's still on those beds, and if you turn off the water now... The best thing we can do is to leave it on until the sun's gone and then pray—and I do mean pray—that no harm's been done. Turn off the water now and we'll lose the whole lot with leaf-burn.'

He was furious with her, scornfully, acidly, bitterly angry, and she couldn't really blame him and yet...and yet...had she been this morning's pretty, flirtatious blonde, she doubted that he would have spoken to her so contemptuously. He was right, though, she ought to have remembered, to have known better, and she dreaded to think what she would have cost her parents if the new crops were damaged. As Carter said, they would just have to pray that no harm had been done.

'I'm going out to put on the sprinklers in the greenhouses,' Carter told her shortly.

'I'll come with you,' she said awkwardly, suddenly anxious to make amends, to prove that she wasn't totally useless, and it hurt her far more than she could have believed possible when he turned in the doorway and told her scathingly,

'Thanks, but no thanks.'

She discovered when he had gone that she was perilously close to tears and that, moreover, her headache had come back with a vengeance. As she went dispiritedly downstairs, somewhere in the distance she heard the first warning rumble of thunder.

That was all she needed, she thought bitterly as she strained her ears, hoping against hope that she had just imagined it. Altogether it had been a horrendous day, and she was only too thankful that it would soon be over. At least if she took herself off to bed with something to read, no more disasters could overtake her, she decided miserably, going into the sitting-room to look along the bookshelves for a suitably soporific novel.

But as she was looking the telephone rang. She picked up the receiver automatically, surprised to hear Peter's voice on the other end of the line.

'Bad news, I'm afraid,' he told her, sounding almost nervous. 'I'm afraid I'm not going to be able to make it this weekend after all.'

CHAPTER NINE

ELSPETH stared disbelievingly at the receiver. 'But Peter, we arranged——'

'Look, I know what we arranged.' He sounded harassed, petulant almost, as though he was both irritated by her and nearly afraid of her. 'But something else has come up. Mother rang me last night. An old friend of the family, my godmother in actual fact, is coming down from Scotland for the weekend and naturally Mother wants me there. She's bringing her daughter with her and, as Mother said, it would almost be an insult to them both if I weren't there, and of course it would hopelessly upset Mother's dinner-table numbers. She's invited the Brigadier round to partner my godmother, and——'

'And you of course will be partnering her daughter,' Elspeth supplied for him, her voice suddenly acid. 'I see. And this, of course, is far more important than being here with me, despite the fact that we arranged this weekend weeks ago, despite the fact that I need you here.'

Silence. She bit down hard on her lip, realising shockingly and furiously that she had been betrayed, that as far as Peter was concerned his mother's wishes, his mother's needs, were far more important than her own, that his loyalty and for all she knew his love lay not with her, but with his mother. It was a galling and extremely unpleasant realisation.

Swallowing her anger, she said as calmly as she could, 'Peter, please, I need you here. I'm sure if you explained to your mother... After all, we *are* virtually on the point of being married—surely my claims on your time, on your——'

She broke off. She could almost see him twitching, uncomfortably guiltily, shifting almost furtively in the chair by his desk.

'It's only one weekend, Elspeth. You know I'm not a country person. Quite honestly I don't see why you needed to go rushing off to Cheshire in the first place, especially since your parents didn't even have the decency to delay their departure until your arrival. If you ask me, that stepcousin of yours or whatever he is has them completely under his thumb. If they lose the entire business it will be their own fault. I tried to warn your father over the phone...'

Elspeth stiffened. This was news to her. 'You did what?' she asked dangerously.

'I've just told you. I tried to warn them, but of course your father wouldn't listen.'

'Peter, we agreed that nothing would be said about that until we had some concrete proof. We agreed.'

'It was for their own benefit, Elspeth. And look, about this weekend—there's really nothing to stop you from coming down to the south coast with me. I'm sure Mother would be delighted.'

'Really? When my presence would put her dinner-table numbers out still further?' Elspeth enquired with acid sweetness. 'Peter, I've never asked you to do anything for me, but I'm asking you now. Please, please come up to Cheshire this weekend as we arranged.'

She told herself that she wasn't testing him or their relationship, that this had nothing to do with Carter or that kiss, nor with the deficiencies she was suddenly seeing in her relationship with Peter... It was simply a matter of knowing where she stood with the man she was going to marry. It was not that she wanted to be more important to him than his mother, it was just—it was just that suddenly and sharply she ached for a little less practicality and a lot more passion.

'Elspeth, don't be ridiculous.' He sounded testy and irritated. 'You *know* I can't. I've already explained to you. Look, once you come back to London we'll——'

'No, Peter,' she interrupted ruthlessly. 'Either you spend this weekend here with me, or our relationship's over.'

There was a silence, and then he blustered, 'Look, Elspeth, this isn't like you, and I'm certainly not going to give in to that kind of blackmail. I can't let Mother down. I can understand that you want me with you.' Was he actually preening himself because of what she had said? Was he actually enjoying refusing her? 'We'll talk about it when you're in a less emotional frame of mind.'

'No, Peter,' she told him steadily. 'We won't talk about it, because I've just realised we no longer have anything to talk about. It's over. Goodbye, Peter.'

And she put the receiver down on him before he could say another word.

It was over; she and Peter were no longer a couple. She was no longer almost engaged, committed. Oddly, she felt neither pain nor relief, only a numbing emptiness, an awareness of a great yawning gap where her future had once been. There would be time later to feel hurt, betrayed, maybe even regret and remorse, but she knew already that there was no going back. That smugness she had heard in Peter's voice, that sureness that he was in the right and that she would see it, that refusal to be aware of her feelings or her needs, had said more than any words. Had there even been a touch of relief behind his smugness when she had thrown that ultimatum at him?

She knew someone who *would* be pleased to hear that their relationship was over. Peter's mother had never made any secret of the fact that she didn't think Elspeth good enough for her only child. No doubt she would far rather see Peter married to some timid, nervous girl whom she could dominate in the same way she had always dominated her husband and son.

She was shivering, Elspeth suddenly realised; and more than that, she felt distinctly odd, quite faint and light-headed.

Somehow or other she made her way back to the kitchen, bumping painfully into the table as she did so, making her way to the sink where she turned on the cold tap and held her wrists beneath its icy flood, hoping the cold water would revive her.

It was the approaching storm that was making her feel so unwell, she told herself stoically, blinking away the tears which had suddenly blurred her vision. Tears of shock, and the pain of discovering that someone she had believed would put her first in his life had actually put her a very poor second. And yet beneath those emotions ran a tiny thread of something else. Relief? Surely not. She had wanted to marry Peter. Less than three days away from him couldn't have changed her so much that now she no longer did so.

Her head was aching unbearably, so much so that she could hardly think. She raised her hand to massage her temples and stiffened with atavistic fear as the distant hills were suddenly illuminated by a forked dart of lightning.

The storm was coming closer. She felt all her old childhood fear returning, intensified by the emotional trauma of recent events, so that her senses were preternaturally heightened and she was unable to exert her normal firm control over her reactions.

She was actually trembling, she realised as she turned on the tap and tried to pour herself a glass of water.

She felt physically **sick** from the pressure inside her head; every instinct she possessed urged her to seek sanctuary somewhere safe and dark, somewhere womblike, she reflected analytically, somewhere where she could escape from her physical pain and be safe from the storm. Somewhere where Peter's defection would no longer hurt—not her heart, she acknowledged sadly, but her pride. It was her pride that was stung by his refusal to put their relationship first. Had she truly loved him? But then she had never... She bit her lip.

Love had never really formed an important part of their relationship. She had liked Peter, admired his determination to succeed in his chosen career, had thought it would be enough for them to have similar goals, similar purposes in life. She had chosen him carefully and she had thought intelligently, and yet the very first time their relationship was tested he had failed her. How would she have felt if she had not made that discovery until after they were married? What was it she really wanted from a man? She closed her eyes, wincing as the thunder rolled closer.

'Close your eyes and think of something nice,' her mother had once urged her compassionately during a particularly bad storm. 'Think of being warm, safe and protected.'

Out of habit more than anything else, she clung to those words now, using them almost like a mantra, but instead of visualising as she normally did somewhere safe and dark where she was protected from the wrath of the storm, the only mental images she had were ones of Carter's arms holding her, Carter's arms protecting her, Carter's voice comforting her.

'No.'

The protest broke from her lips as she wrenched herself away from the temptation of her own thoughts. Her heart was thumping far too quickly, and not just from fear—or at least not fear of the storm. Was this why she had felt that tiny thread of release at the ending of her relationship with

Peter? Because of Carter? Because of a man whom she knew to be untrustworthy, and yet who nevertheless aroused her in ways which she had thought in her ignorance belonged only to teenagers and the fevered imaginations of certain novelists?

Carter—where was he? Why didn't he come back? The sky had filled with black clouds, the thunder rumbled closer, drawn, she suspected, by the awesome mystery of The Edge—that strange, magical place where locals said no birds ever sang and where Merlin was supposed to haunt the underground caverns.

She shivered violently, the tiny hairs on her arms lifting in frightened awareness of the force of the coming storm. She was trembling so much she could hardly move. When Carter came back—— She tensed, remembering how furious he had been with her, how contemptuous. No doubt when he came in and discovered her standing shivering with fright, and all because of a thunderstorm, he would be doubly contemptuous. She caught sight of a bottle of her mother's elderberry wine standing on the dresser.

Perhaps a glass of that might steady her nerves a little. She walked across the kitchen and on the third attempt managed to pour some of the pale liquid into her glass. The glass she had picked up was the one she had used for her drink of water, and she had perhaps rather overfilled it, she recognised, taking a deep gulp.

The wine was instantly warming, relaxing the tensed muscles of her throat, filling the empty space inside her with pleasant heat. She could almost feel it unlocking her over-tensed nerves, Elspeth decided, carefully carrying both the glass and the bottle over to the table and slumping into one of the chairs.

Common sense told her that she really ought to go upstairs and get into bed, where she could bury her head under the bedclothes and blot out the storm, but she felt strangely reluctant to leave the kitchen; almost as though something was making her stay, making her wait—for what?

For Carter.

She took another quick gulp of the wine, trying desperately to ignore what her own brain was telling her.

Of course she wasn't waiting for Carter. Why on earth should she be? He meant nothing to her, nothing at all, other than the fact that he might be trying to destroy her parents' business. That was her only interest in him, of course it was. And if when he had kissed her she had just happened to react . . . well, then all that proved was that—that he was an extremely seductive and dangerous man, she thought bitterly, staring in some confusion into her almost empty glass.

Had she really drunk that full glass of wine? She could only remember taking the first two gulps. Now the glass was virtually empty. It was true that there was a delicious warm feeling in the pit of her stomach, she acknowledged, focusing with some difficulty.

It was also true that her headache had started to recede a little. Perhaps if she had a little more wine it might go altogether. It seemed extraordinarily difficult to fill up her glass. For some reason it kept on moving. In fact the entire room was swaying very gently around her, almost as though they were at sea. The threatening crash of the thunder was getting closer. The storm was going to pass right overhead, Elspeth recognised, shivering as her fear broke through the wine-induced haze. She heard someone moaning, a sharp, high-pitched sound, and stared wildly round the kitchen, wondering if she had imagined the noise—and then realised that she herself had made it.

In the corner, Jasper the parrot was whistling to himself, apparently oblivious to the storm. Elspeth winced as lightning tore jaggedly at the sky, and quickly took another deep gulp of her wine. It certainly seemed to be helping; she certainly felt less terror than normal. Her fear was still there, but the wine had distanced her from it. Was she perhaps just a little bit tipsy? she asked herself uneasily, suddenly aware of how very uncoordinated her movements had become. Surely not. She very rarely drank, and she certainly never got—tipsy. But perhaps she had better not drink any more. Peter didn't approve of women who drank. Tears of self-pity filled her eyes and slid down her face. She tried to brush them away and missed.

The storm was getting closer—too close. She was just beginning to feel the old familiar terror gathering force inside her, when the back door suddenly opened and Carter came in.

She tried to stand up, which she told herself later was her first big mistake. Why on earth she thought she ought to stand up, she had no idea, only that it seemed as though Carter was towering over her, glowering down at her, as he looked first at her tear-blotched face and then at the glass and bottle.

'What the devil...?'

Sensitive to his anger, Elspeth immediately flared up. What right had he to dictate to her what she could or could not do? She told him so in a husky, confused sentence which somehow or other became very jumbled and which she hastily concluded, saying crossly, 'And anyway, why shouldn't I have a glass of wine if I want one?' Not for anything was she going to tell him why she had drunk it.

'A glass,' Carter retorted scathingly. 'You've damn near drunk the whole bottle. Have you no idea how potent that stuff is? My God. What would your precious Peter say if he could see you now.'

To her own horror Elspeth felt huge tears start to roll down her face. 'He isn't mine any longer,' she choked back at him. 'It's over.'

There was a moment's silence, and then Carter demanded grimly, 'What?'

'You heard me,' Elspeth told him recklessly. 'It's over. Peter and I are no longer. It seems that his mother's wishes are more important to him than mine; that he'd rather spend the weekend with her, entertaining her friends, than here with me. And he knew how much I wanted him here. How important it was to me.' She sniffed and then winced as lightning forked across the fields, her whole body stiffening as she stared outside, unable to drag her terrified gaze away.

'Elspeth.' Carter's voice suddenly changed, lost its impatient, angry tone and instead, incredibly, became gentle, tender almost. 'It's all right, the storm won't hurt you. You're safe in here. Look...'

Elspeth turned her head and tried to focus on him, struggling to bring her thoughts to some kind of order, trying to clear the drink-induced miasma from her brain.

'I know you're frightened of storms,' Carter was saying quietly. 'Your mother told me.' He saw her expression, and his own mouth suddenly became very grim. 'For God's sake, what kind of man do you think I am? Don't you think I have any compassion, any understanding? It's been a bad day all round for you, hasn't it? First Peter, and now this.' He reached out and touched her face gently with his fingertips and she had an insane desire to lean into him and on to him, to simply let him take charge, to...

'Look, why don't you go upstairs and get into bed. I'll bring you up a cup of tea. I can understand why you did this,' he added wryly, picking up the wine bottle. 'But it really isn't the answer.'

Did he actually think she had deliberately got drunk?

'It was a mistake,' she told him huskily. 'The glass. I didn't realise...'

Her thoughts had become extremely muddled—chaotically so, and she was finding it impossible to concentrate on anything other than how wonderful Carter looked, and how much she would like him to take her in his arms right now and kiss her the way he had done before. He was looking right at her and with such a strange expression on his face that for one moment she thought she had actually given voice to that desire, but then she heard him saying curtly, 'I think we'd better get you upstairs, and then——'

Just as she was protesting that she could manage, the thunder rolled noisily overhead, followed by the unmistakable sound of glass breaking.

'Damn—that must be one of the greenhouses. I'd better go out and check the damage. You stay right where you are,' he told Elspeth as she tried to get up. 'I'll be as quick as I can.'

He heard her gasp as lightning forked brilliantly outside and turned to look at her. 'Elspeth.'

She shook her head, fighting to clear her fogged brain. 'I'm all right,' she lied huskily. 'You go and check on the greenhouse.' She'd never forgive herself if more damage than necessary was caused through her inability to cope with her stupid fear. She could see that Carter was reluctant to leave her, but they both knew that the greenhouse was more important than her dread of the storm.

'Well, stay right where you are,' Carter told her a second time, as he opened the back door. 'I'll be as quick as I can.'

But once he was gone, she couldn't stay in the kitchen any longer—and besides, what did she need his help for? All she needed was to be somewhere dark and safe. Somewhere where the storm couldn't reach her and where she could give in to the need to close her eyes.

It took her quite some time to weave her way across the kitchen and to open the door, but at last she managed it, climbing the stairs with slow precision and then making her way very carefully along the landing to her bedroom.

She found the bed without having to switch on the light, and then paused, hesitating before dropping down on to it, frowning in concentration as she fought with the zipper on her jeans, finally managing to struggle out of them and to remove her top. Her underwear quickly followed and was left to lie carelessly on the floor, something she would never normally have dreamed of doing, but her head was spinning so much and she felt so very, very tired.

In fact, in the act of searching for her nightdress she stopped and yawned hugely, promptly forgetting what it was she had been about to do as she half climbed and half stumbled into the middle of the bed, only just managing to push back the duvet, and then quickly burrowing beneath it, pulling it right up over her ears and using it to blot out the sounds of the storm outside.

'Elspeth. Elspeth, wake up.'

Someone was shaking her, trying to wake her up, when she didn't want to be woken up. She said as much, protesting sleepily, and then abruptly making the delicious discovery that the hands firmly trying to shake her awake were attached to arms, and that those arms felt absolutely wonderful beneath her exploring fingertips ... smooth, hard, and so very strong, she could even feel the muscles in them contracting beneath her tentative exploration, an awareness that made her feel extremely powerful and rather triumphant until she realised that they were being moved away from her.

She muttered a protest and clung, wriggling closer.

'Elspeth.'

This time the voice was right in her ear, making her wince and frown. It was a very nice voice, she decided, refusing to open her eyes, even if it did sound rather cross, and the sensation of it so close to her ear was sending the most delicious spirals of sensation over her skin; so delicious in fact that she felt it only fair to show her appreciation, which she promptly did by burying her face in the lovely warm angle between Carter's neck and shoulder, experimentally nibbling at his bare skin. It tasted even better than she had dreamed, so very, very good, in fact, that she couldn't resist nibbling her way up to his ear, where she told him sleepily, 'Mmm ... Carter, this is really nice. I wish you would hold me properly though and kiss me,' she added reproachfully.

She felt the hiss of his indrawn breath and then the tension invade his body.

'*You* are drunk,' he told her flatly. 'And what's more you're in my bed.'

Now she did open her eyes, propping herself up on one elbow as she withdrew from him in affronted dignity. He was, she saw with some pleasure, undressed, and was obviously about to get into bed.

Her bed. She had been right about that. She recognised the shadowy shape of the room and the position of the window.

She told him as much, virtuously keeping her eyes on his face instead of letting her gaze wander, as it very much wished to do, over the exposed expanse of his chest. It was a pity, she decided regretfully, that the room's shadows cloaked the rest of him, because she was sure that he had the kind of body that she would find it very pleasurable indeed to look at.

Oddly, it didn't strike her as the least bit strange that she should be thinking of behaving in such a way, and as for Carter's allegation that she was drunk... Impossible, she never drank. She dismissed a hazy recollection of her mother's elderberry wine and a very large tumbler and instead concentrated on her victory.

'This is my room,' she reaffirmed.

'Yes,' Carter agreed grimly. 'But at the moment *I* happen to be sleeping in it. *You* are sleeping in your parents'.'

Elspeth's forehead furrowed. 'Not. I'm not—I'm sleeping here, or at least I was until you woke me up.'

'Well, now that you're awake, do you suppose you could get out of my bed and go and sleep in your own?' Carter rasped, patently unmollified.

Elspeth blinked owlishly at him. He really was getting rather cross, and as far as she could see there wasn't any need. 'It's all right, Carter,' she told him in a kind voice, patting the empty space beside her. 'There's plenty of room in here for both of us.'

'What? Oh, for God's sake don't be so stupid. I can't sleep with you. I don't want to.'

Elspeth froze. No, of course, he didn't want to. Just like Peter hadn't wanted to. She wasn't desirable enough, attractive enough.

She said as much to him, sitting up in bed, her chin firming proudly, completely oblivious to the fact that a watery moon had broken through the clouds and was shedding a faint silver light into the room so that her body was illuminated in its translucent gleam, her breasts pale and full and tipped with small, hard nipples.

'Elspeth,' Carter groaned despairingly.

'No, please don't make me go,' she whispered. 'Please, Carter, let me stay. I don't want to be on my own. Not tonight.'

'If you stay I'll make love to you,' Carter warned her savagely.

'I want you to,' Elspeth told him shakily. 'In fact I think I've wanted to ever since—ever since you kissed me down by the stream.'

'This is madness—complete madness,' she heard him saying thickly, but it didn't stop him from leaning towards her, and slowly, so slowly that it was more of an adoration than a mere caress, he ran his hands up over her body, from the curve of her hips to the softness of her breasts, pausing briefly there, while her breath locked in her throat and her heart pounded with sledgehammer beats and then his hands moved on, cupping the rounded ball of each shoulder. He leaned forward and kissed her, a questioning, delicate kiss that did little more than brush the softness of her lips, but she trembled so violently under it that both of them stilled.

'You really want this?' Carter demanded against her lips.

She couldn't speak. Could only nod her head, her eyes huge and brilliant, her body achingly aware that, with his, it could learn pleasures so intense that they would never be forgotten.

He kissed her again, his mouth hard, the kiss brief, and then again and again, until their mouths fused in hot, eager need and this time when his hands touched her body it was with the sure, knowledgeable touch of a lover, stroking, enticing, exciting, making her gasp beneath his mouth and arch under his hands as they kneeled body to body in the moonlight.

Her own hands, more skilled, more knowing, more wanton than she had ever dreamed they could be, stroked him, told him how much they delighted in the pleasure of this intimacy with him.

When he buried his mouth in the soft curve of her throat, she arched eagerly against him, her breasts pressed flat against his chest, her nipples sensitised by the quickening movements of his body.

When he laid her down on the bed, she gazed at him in wondering delight, aching to be able to find the words to tell him how he made her feel.

But it seemed that words were unnecessary and that her trembling flesh silently conveyed to him its pleasure in his touch by responding quiveringly to the exquisite sensations aroused first by his hands and then by his mouth.

When his tongue-tip traced the aureole of her breast she shuddered wildly and clung to him, gasping his name, her whole body tensing in spasms of white-hot pleasure when he responded to her need by opening his mouth over her tight, hard nipple and then by suckling on it with increasing urgency.

Elspeth had never dreamed herself capable of such wild abandonment, of such fevered, aching need, of such instinctive, overwhelming sensuality, as she opened her body to him, and wrapped herself around him, her mouth trembling, burning where it touched his skin, eager to absorb the taste and texture of him. Gone were the restraints of the past. This was where she wanted to be—where she needed to be.

She felt no self-consciousness, no guilt, no hesitation . . . only an overwhelming knowledge of the rightness of what she was doing.

It was as great a pleasure to touch Carter, to stroke and taste him, to feel his body shudder with reciprocal desire when she did so, as it was to have him touching her. It was like having a banquet of delights spread out in front of her, she thought dizzily, nuzzling his throat and then his shoulder, exploring the indentation of his spine and then the hard, flat plane of his buttocks, her body thrilling with awareness of the aroused heat and weight of him against her.

'Elspeth, you don't know what you're doing to me,' he told her thickly in between kisses.

'I know what you're doing to me,' she whispered shakily, watching his eyes go dark as his hand stroked her body and felt its betraying tremble. He was touching her so gently, so intimately, so pleasurably that there was nothing she could do other than give herself up to the voluptuous, velvet darkness of that pleasure, unable to stop him even when she felt the mind-destroying lap of his tongue against the most intimate part of her body and knew shockingly that there was nothing she wanted more than to return the intimacy of that caress, unless it was the fully aroused heat of him deep within her body, easing that tormenting ache that the soft stroke of his tongue was deliberately arousing.

She told him so, unaware of the jumbled litany of praise and pleas that left her lips, knowing only that his arousal, his desire were suddenly tumultuously urgent and that he, like her, seemed to know instinctively that her quivering body needed to feel him deep within its softness.

The sensation of him being there, the careful tenderness with which he controlled his body's powerful surge, the way in which he held her, gentled her and held back his own pleasure while he shepherded hers, filled her with such emotion, such joy—such love, she recognised, her mind and flesh suddenly free of any kind of self-deceit—that she opened herself willingly and eagerly to him, and the passage of his flesh within her own was so acutely pleasurable that she met each thrust with trembling eagerness, letting the forces inside her gather and coalesce until they couldn't be contained any longer.

She cried out in the first white heat of shattering release, felt herself fall through space into the safety of Carter's arms as the initial sharp dazzle of pleasure left her boneless and fluid.

She could hear Carter breathing heavily, feel his body trembling slightly in the aftermath of his own release. He was still holding her, stroking her damp skin, whispering soft words to her that she was too exhausted to hear.

All at once she felt hugely tired, so physically relaxed that it was impossible to move, impossible to do anything other than turn into the warmth of Carter's body, nuzzle his throat appreciatively and then fall deeply asleep as she snuggled deeper into his embrace.

CHAPTER TEN

'I've brought you a cup of tea.'

Elspeth shuddered wildly as she recognised Carter's voice. Her head was pounding, her mouth felt sour and dry, her stomach was churning nauseously, but worst of all the sound of Carter's voice had brought an effortless and total recall of the events of the previous night.

The fact that she was now in her parents' bed and not her own did not provide any reassurance that she had simply dreamed the whole appalling incident. For one thing, she doubted that her imagination was that good. For another, every time she moved there were unfamiliar aches and tensions within her body which she was quite sure had nothing to do with the pounding in her head or the nausea in her stomach.

Tea. It was the last thing she wanted. No, Carter's presence in her bedroom reminding her of what she had done—that was the last thing she wanted.

She wished there were some way she could block out forever her all too vivid memories of the way she had seduced—there really was no other word for it—Carter. A faint moan escaped involuntarily from her tight throat. She opened her eyes just in time to see Carter hurriedly putting down the cup and advancing towards the bed.

Foolishly, in view of what had happened, she clutched hold of the bedclothes as though in terror of having them ripped from her, shrinking back under them, while Carter came to an abrupt halt, his face blenching.

'I've got to go and check on the greenhouses, see if there's been any more damage.'

She nodded her head, her throat too tight to allow her to speak. She wished he would go and leave her if not in peace, then at least in privacy to digest the unappetising memories of her wanton behaviour.

It was the drink, of course. There could be no other explanation, and everyone knew that strong alcohol could have the strangest effect on those not used to drinking it. Which was why, of course, sensible mothers advised their teenage daughters to treat it with great caution.

Carter seemed strangely reluctant to leave her room. He had walked over to the window and was standing staring out of it. This morning he was dressed in jeans and a long-sleeved cotton shirt. He turned round abruptly and where the collar lay open she saw a small dark mark, like a bruise, just above his collarbone. She stared at it like someone transfixed, her colour coming and going.

Had *she* done that? Vague, unnerving images filtered through her aching brain. She remembered clutching on to Carter's arms, digging her nails into his hard muscles, telling him in frantic whispers how much she had wanted to touch and taste him.

A small whimper of protest bubbled in her throat. Numbly she pulled the beclothes over her head.

She heard Carter sigh, a small, explosive sound. Of what? Anger? Irritation? Amusement? After all, he hadn't stopped her, had he? Oh, no, he had let her go right ahead and make a complete fool of herself. And he could have stopped her . . . couldn't he? He could have refused. Refused to what? Allow her to arouse him? Would she have wanted that? Would she have been feeling any better this morning if she were confronting the knowledge that he had rejected her? At least last night had proved to her that she was capable of arousing a man to desire, that not all men were as cold as Peter. But to have made love with a man—no, she corrected herself sharply, not *with* a man, but to a man—for no other reason than to prove she could arouse him to desire . . . How truly appalling. But no more appalling surely than to have got drunk and then made sexual advances to a man with whom one was secretly and very desperately in love.

In love. *She*, in love with Carter. How ridiculous—how impossible. Anyway, she didn't believe in falling in love. She was far too mature, far too sensible. Mature—a woman of her age who made love without even stopping to think of taking any kind of precautions against pregnancy or anything else.

'Elspeth,' she heard Carter saying urgently. 'We've got to talk.'

Talk. That was the last thing she wanted to do.

'Go away,' she moaned from beneath the bedclothes. 'Please, just go away.'

Perhaps he could hear the hysteria she was only just keeping at bay, or perhaps he was really as appalled by the whole thing as she was herself and eager only to escape, to make it plain to her that last night was an aberration, that it meant nothing. Well, there was no need for him to reinforce that truth to her. She was quite prepared to take the blame, to admit that the whole thing had been her fault. And if he thought that she was the kind of woman who believed that just because he had been her first lover, just because she might be carrying his child, just because she was quite despairingly and hopelessly in love with him, it meant that he owed her anything at all, she would soon show him that she wasn't.

She waited until she was sure he was gone before peering over the bedclothes. Outside the sky was a soft grey. The storm was over—her whole life was over, she thought mournfully, getting out of bed and staggering sickly as she felt the full impact of last night's bottle of elderberry wine. Elderberry wine—what on earth had possessed her? It wasn't even as though she didn't know how strong it was.

In the bathroom, she suppressed a strong desire to be extremely unwell and searched feverishly through her mother's cabinet for something to subdue the riot in her head and stomach.

Finding nothing, she made do with cleaning her teeth with enough vigour to make her head ache even further, having a shower, washing her hair, acknowledging that it was too likely that she wouldn't even be able to keep an aspirin down and making herself a promise that the first thing she was going to do was to drive to the village and buy herself some Alka Seltzer.

Driving her car down the bumpy lane was a form of self-inflicted torture that made her vow she would never touch another drop of alcohol in her life. She parked her car in the village and climbed out cautiously. The pain in her head had reached catastrophic proportions, and she was only thankful that her poor eyes weren't forced to endure the bright light of the sun.

She had almost reached the chemist when someone stopped her, a bright female voice calling her name. She turned round, recognising one of the girls she had been at school with.

She had two small children in tow and she grinned happily when she saw Elspeth. 'My goodness, what on earth's the matter with you?' she asked anxiously, seeing Elspeth's white face.

'Hangover,' Elspeth admitted unwillingly, wincing as Louise laughed.

'You? I don't believe it. Weren't you the one who virtuously refused to join in when we all drank that bottle of cider behind the bike sheds?'

'Yes—more's the pity. If I had done, I'd have had more sense than to get myself in this state.'

'Did—er—Carter join you in this revelry?' her friend enquired dulcetly.

Elspeth shot her an acid look. She and Louise had once been close friends, and still kept in touch. She had been Louise's senior bridesmaid when she'd married Allen, and she was godmother to both her girls.

'Carter?' she repeated with what she hoped was convincing disinterest.

'Yes. He *is* staying at your folks' place, isn't he? Allen said he was bidding at yesterday's auction. He got the old Thatchford place, didn't he, and those fields next to your parents? Which reminds me—did seeing him again stir up any of those wanton teenage yearnings?' She giggled conspiratorially. 'Remember how both of us used to drool over him that summer your aunt first brought him here?'

Elspeth, who had been concentrating solely on the news Louise had just given her, looked at her friend and snapped defensively, 'You may have drooled—I never did. I disliked him. I always have.'

'Oh, come on. I know that was what you liked to pretend, but we both know the truth. Remember how I caught you writing his name all over the front of your maths rough-book, and drawing hearts all over the place with his initials on them. You were crazy about him. We both were. Remember how we used to wonder what it would be like if he kissed us. My God, when I look at these two and remember what I've got to go through I start thinking I ought to lock them up in a nunnery. How's Peter, by the way? You two set a date yet?'

'No—nor are we going to,' Elspeth told her shortly, ignoring her friend's surprise and pressing her hand to her aching head.

'Look, why don't you come back with me and have a cup of coffee?'

She wanted to refuse but Louise refused to let her, and there was something rather comforting about letting Louise bully her affectionately, treating her almost in the same way as she did her two small daughters.

And besides, if she went home with Louise it would mean that she needn't face Carter—at least not yet.

She spent an hour with Louise and her family, at the end of which the Alka Seltzer Louise had given her had started to take effect. She felt decidedly better, and having resolutely refused to acknowledge Louise's teasing comments about her teenage crush on Carter, she realised now that even if she had deliberately forgotten it and even denied it, Louise was quite right. She had had the most mammoth crush on Carter, had indeed dreamed and drooled over him and had even, she blushed to recall, written his name all over her maths book.

You might be able to deceive yourself, she reflected grimly, as she drove home, but you certainly couldn't deceive an old friend, especially not one who had shared your growing years with you.

But she had more urgent things to dwell on than her own folly. Louise's revelation that Carter had bought those fields had really jolted her. She had managed to push to the back of her mind Peter's allegations against him, but now suddenly she was forced to confront them.

She drove slowly down the lane and then into the yard.

As she did so the back door opened and Carter erupted into the yard. He looked furiously angry, so angry in fact that for a moment she almost decided not to get out of the car. And then she reminded herself that this was *her* home—well, at least her parents' home—that Carter was the intruder, and that, even worse, he was deliberately setting out to ruin her parents, and that gave her the strength to push open her door and get out.

She had scarcely put one foot on the ground before Carter suddenly grabbed hold of her and virtually yanked her out of her car. He was almost shaking her as he demanded to know where she had been, and yet oddly instead of feeling frightened she experienced a strange, dizzying sense of exhilaration.

'Just where the hell have you been?' he was demanding as he shook her. 'If you think I'm going to let you walk out on me and back to him after last night——'

'I didn't walk anywhere,' Elspeth interrupted him. 'I drove to the village to buy some Alka Seltzer.'

'You *drove*—in your condition? Are you mad? Don't you realise you could still be over the limit? My God, have you no sense?'

For a moment Elspeth was too stunned to speak, and then she fired back bitterly, 'I might not have any sense, but at least I have some morals. At least I'm not trying to destroy someone—at least I'm not trying to steal from them. How could you buy those fields when you know my parents need them? Peter was right—you've been out to cheat my parents all along. You bought those fields so that you can put them out of business.'

Ridiculously she was suddenly close to tears, unbearably hating knowing that after all Peter had been right. It didn't stop her loving Carter—nothing could do that, she recognised dismally. Carter stared at her, his mouth thinning.

'Are you crazy? I don't believe I'm hearing any of this. I bought those fields, not for myself, but for your parents—on their behalf, in fact. My God, how could you suspect...? And to think that last night I actually thought you were finally beginning to realise. But it's all Peter with you, isn't it? Nothing else—*no one* else exists,' he demanded bitterly. 'Well, I don't know what kind of rules you live by, Elspeth, but the ones I live by don't include one-night stands. When I make love to a woman, even when she's doing the asking,' he added mercilessly, 'it's because I've already made some kind of emotional commitment to her, because I want far more from her than the brief pleasure of her body. OK, so now you're going to tell me that it only happened because you've lost Peter, that you were using me as a substitute for him, but let me tell you this: no woman makes love to a man the way you did to me without feeling something, and you knew damn well it wasn't Peter you were holding in your arms last night. You knew damn well it wasn't Peter you wanted to kiss and hold you. It wasn't Peter's body you wanted——'

'Stop,' Elspeth demanded huskily, and then asked, 'Did you really buy those fields for my parents?'

He gave her a hard look and said tersely, 'I'm not after their business. I'm thinking of a much larger market than theirs—supplying super-markets. I've already had some interest shown and I believe I can make a go of it. The reason I chose Cheshire was because of you—you, Elspeth—you! Yes, but if you don't believe me——'

She shook her head. Too much was happening too quickly. She felt as though she were falling helplessly through space with no one to help her. 'Last night,' she began huskily, but Carter wouldn't let her finish.

'Last night,' he told her ruthlessly, 'you asked me to make love to you and I did what any man— any normal man who's spent far too many years crazy about a particular woman would do when that same woman whispers to him that she wants and needs him. I lost control. And you may as well know that I don't regret a moment of it. All right, so it doesn't matter to you that I've wasted years of my life just aching for a chance to show you how I feel about you, it doesn't matter that it was me who held you last night, who *pleasured* you, loved you. What the hell is it that he's got and I don't have, Elspeth, apart from your love? I love you, for God's sake, while he . . .'

Elspeth swayed giddily. 'You love me?'

'Of course I do, dammit!' Carter bellowed. 'When your parents told me that they thought you were getting tired of your high-profile city life, that they felt that you wanted to come home, I thought, at last, here's my chance. I was on the verge of leaving the institute anyway, and I thought, where better to settle down than in Cheshire, so that I could be near you, so that I could have a chance to show you——' He broke off, shaking his head. 'When we first met you were too young, just a girl. I couldn't tell you.'

'Carter,' Elspeth demanded shakily. 'Can you think of something you could do to prove to me that I'm not imagining all this?'

Something in her voice must have alerted him to the truth. He looked at her and tensed. A muscle twitched briefly in his jaw and then he was coming towards her, taking hold of her, wrapping her in his arms, his voice husky and just a little bit uncertain as he asked against her mouth, 'How about this?'

Hours, or was it only seconds later, Elspeth drew away from him, convinced now beyond any doubt that he loved her just as compulsively as she was beginning to realise she loved him, and probably had loved him for a very long time, if she had only had the wit to realise it.

'Carter?' she asked him, fiddling with the buttons on his shirt. 'Last night, did you really...?' She whispered something into his ear and blushed as he looked at her and said softly,

'Yes. Why?'

'Nothing. Well, it's just...my memories of last night are a tiny bit hazy, and I was wondering. Do you think you could do it again?' she asked him breathlessly.

'I see. Some lover, aren't I, if you've forgotten what it felt like already?' he said drily.

She smiled dreamily at him. 'Oh, no, I haven't forgotten. I just wanted to see if it was actually as wonderful as I remember.'

'Well, Mrs MacDonald, is it still as wonderful as you remember?' Carter teased his wife of exactly fifteen months as she lay contentedly in his arms, in the shadowed peace of their bedroom.

Their two-month-old son had been taken firmly in charge by his grandmother, who had announced that it was time that his doting parents had a little time to themselves.

'Mmm. I'm not sure.' Elspeth wriggled blissfully closer to him, pretending to consider, laughter gleaming in her eyes as she suggested thoughtfully, 'I don't suppose you could do it again, could you? Carter! Carter!' she protested, laughing, as her husband proceeded to show her that he most assuredly could.